THE ENGLISHMAN'S
BRIDE

THE ENGLISHMAN'S BRIDE

BY
SOPHIE WESTON

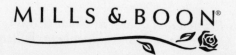

First published in Great Britain 2001
Large Print edition 2002
Harlequin Mills & Boon Limited,
Eton House, 18-24 Paradise Road,
Richmond, Surrey TW9 1SR

© Sophie Weston 2001

ISBN 0 263 17305 4

Set in Times Roman 15½ on 16½ pt.
16-0602-53198

Printed and bound in Great Britain
by Antony Rowe Ltd, Chippenham, Wiltshire

PROLOGUE

THE Englishman was deceptive. Even after twenty-four hours, every man in the detachment agreed on that. He might look like a Hollywood heartthrob with his wild midnight hair and haughty profile. But the tall, thin body was as lithe as a cat. And he was tireless.

When they first heard that a New York bureaucrat was joining them on their jungle expedition, they muttered resentfully. But when they learned that he was a member of the British aristocracy as well, they nearly mutinied.

'*Sir* Philip Hardesty?' queried Texas Joe, stunned.

'I ain't calling no snotty pen-pusher "Sir",' said Spanners. As an Englishman himself, he spoke with authority.

The group decided to take their line from Spanners. And when the man arrived they were sure they were right. As well as his title, Philip Hardesty possessed beautifully kept hands, a backpack that was so new it shone and customised jungle boots.

But he did not use his title. He got his hands dirty without noticing it. When they waded through the river his boots kept the water out better than their own. And there was that tireless determination.

Nothing got him down. Not the evil-smelling insect repellent. Not the stifling humidity. Not the long, exhausting days pushing on through the jungle. Not even the horrible nights.

He did not have their precision training but his endurance was phenomenal. In his quiet way, he was as strong as any of them. He took the long days without complaint. He climbed well when he had to. And when he swung that bulky new pack off his back at rest stops, you could see that his shoulders were dense with muscle.

All right, none of them had wanted a civilian along. Captain Soames had wanted him least of all, though of course he had not said so. The trip was dangerous enough, between the hazards of the jungle and the unpredictable moods of the so-called freedom fighters that they were coming to see.

But High Command had insisted. And for once High Command had been right.

The man even knew how to make a fire—and how to put it out.

'How did you get into this line of work?' said Captain Soames as they all sat round the small flames.

It was their last night before they reached the rebels' camp. All six of the men who had volunteered for this duty knew that there was no forecasting what awaited them at the camp. Rafek, the rebel leader, said he wanted to talk. It was he who had made the first contact. But rebels had lied before.

Philip Hardesty said quietly, 'Family tradition.'

'Very British,' said Australian Captain Soames drily. 'How long has the UN been going? Remind me.'

Philip Hardesty smiled. 'Hardestys were meddling in other people's affairs long before the UN thought of it. We've been doing it for centuries.'

It was a smile you remembered. It seemed to light a candle inside a mask. You had been talking to him, getting nothing but impassive logic back—and then he smiled!

Suddenly you felt he had opened a window to you. You could read him! And he was friendly! You felt you had been given a present.

'I bet you're good at it,' said the hard-bitten captain, warming to Philip Hardesty in spite of recognising how the trick was done.

'There's no point in doing something if you don't do it well.'

'I'll vote for that,' the captain agreed. 'So your family are OK with this?'

There was a tiny pause.

'No family. Ancestors, yes. Family, no.'

'Oh.' The captain was genuinely surprised.

The wonderful smile died. 'Families need commitment,' said Philip Hardesty levelly. 'I can't do that.'

The captain shuffled uncomfortably. Sometimes, on these small, dangerous expeditions, men confided stuff that later they wished they hadn't. He didn't want to be the keeper of Philip Hardesty's conscience.

But the man was not talking about his conscience, it seemed.

He said unemotionally, 'You see, the job of a negotiator—a good negotiator—is to see everyone's point of view. To say, no one is ever wholly in the wrong. Peace is just a matter of finding enough room for everyone to have some of what they want.'

The captain was puzzled. 'So?'

'So lack of commitment is my greatest professional asset. The moment I lose that, I'm in the soup. With everybody else trying to reach some goal of his own, I have to stay absolutely without any goals at all.'

The captain thought it over.

'But surely personal stuff is different—'

'Not for me,' said Philip Hardesty, cool and level and just a little weary. 'I can't live two lives. What I am, I am all the way through.'

The captain thought, And maybe that's why this bastard we're going to see tomorrow trusts him.

'And that's why you don't have a family? I see. Seems a lot to give up.'

Philip shrugged. 'Family tradition,' he said again.

The captain hesitated. But the others were either on watch or asleep and confidences seemed to be the order of the day.

'Isn't that lonely?' he asked curiously.

The jungle night was full of noises. Above their heads, a bat screeched. There was a whirr of wings as some predator took off after it.

Philip held his hands out to the fire, though the night was not cold and the fire was dying.

'Lonely?' he echoed. 'All the time.'

Five days later, Captain Soames was responding to reporters in the makeshift conference room at Pelanang airstrip.

Yes, they'd all got out alive. Yes, it had been dangerous. Yes, that part of the jungle was uncharted. Yes, they had brought back some totally new specimens.

'And now we're going to publish the map. Which was the aim of the expedition in the first place.'

'You took UN negotiator Sir Philip Hardesty along with you on a field trip?' said the local stringer for a group of European newspapers, scenting a story. 'Do you want to comment on that?'

'Sure,' said Captain Soames with a grin. 'It was a privilege.'

But later, over a beer under the palm trees, he said, 'The Englishman? Off the record? The guy's a phenomenon. If anyone can get these lunatics to make peace, he can.'

'What's he like?' said the stringer, intrigued. 'I mean, as a person.'

Captain Soames lowered the beer can. His face was sober.

'As a person? He's the loneliest man in the world.'

CHAPTER ONE

'ANOTHER satisfied customer,' said Mrs Ludwig, pushing the envelope across the desk. 'They wanted you to stay on, of course. Don't they always?'

'That's nice of them,' said Kit Romaine, pocketing her salary envelope without opening it.

Really, the way that girl ignored money was downright heathen, thought Mrs Ludwig.

She said curiously, 'Aren't you ever tempted?'

'To stay on in one job?' Kit shook her head. 'I like my freedom.'

She more than liked it. She needed it. It had taken her a long time to work that out. Now she had, she was hanging on to it like a drowning man to a lifeboat.

Mrs Ludwig shook her head. 'From our point of view that's fine, of course. You're probably the best temp we've got. But shouldn't you be thinking of your future?'

'I'm strictly a live-for-today kind of girl,' said Kit firmly. She had learned that the hard way too.

Mrs Ludwig gave up. She looked swiftly down her list.

'Well, next week there's a complete spring clean of a house in Pimlico. Owners moving back in after tenants. You'd like that. You'd have the place to yourself. Or Henderson's Books need cover while their under-manager goes to a book fair. They particularly asked for you, by the way. Oh, no, that's next month. Oh, hang on—there's the Bryants again.' She caught herself. 'No, that won't do, you'd have to look after the little girl after school for a couple of hours.'

In spite of what she said, she looked up questioningly. The Bryants were good clients. She'd like to give them the best. In terms of competence and reliability, Kit Romaine was the best.

But Kit Romaine was shaking her blonde head vigorously. Kit Romaine did not look after children. It was the only thing she refused to do.

This Century's Solutions was a London agency priding itself on being able to find someone to solve any problem, no matter how extraordinary. Kit met the job description brilliantly. She was fit, clear-headed and completely unflappable. She was as at home with an embroidery frame as she was with a computer. Assignments that other people regarded as hopeless were just a challenge to Kit.

'If there's a problem, there's a solution,' she would say serenely. And take herself off to the library to research the problem of the moment.

There were only two things that Kit Romaine did not do. She wouldn't take care of children. And she didn't date.

Which was odd when you came to think of it. A gorgeous girl like that: good figure, perfect skin and the sort of grace that made people turn and look at her in the street. A client had even wanted to use her in a television commercial once. It was a shame to waste all that long, silky blonde hair, or so he had said. Kit had laughed at him. And been adamant in her refusal.

Make that three things that Kit Romaine did not do, thought Mrs Ludwig, sighing.

'Not the Bryants,' Kit was saying now. 'Give me the house-cleaning. A whole week should get me to the end of module ten.'

Mrs Ludwig laughed. 'What is it this time?'

'War poetry.'

Mrs Ludwig pulled a face.

'Sounds grim. Rather you than me.'

'It's not all grim, actually. It's stuff every educated person ought to know.'

Kit was a dedicated self-educator. When she worked alone, she would slap a tape of her most recent subject into her Walkman. Then she could clean or drive or groom or do whatever it was she was being paid to do. And all the time, as she explained to Helen Ludwig, she was increasing her knowledge.

Helen Ludwig, who had two degrees and generally forgot both of them, wrote it off as an eccentricity. It did not get in the way of Kit's efficiency or the agency reputation, and that was all she cared about.

'Whatever you say,' she said, bored. 'The Pimlico house it is. Pick up the keys here on Monday.'

Kit nodded and stood up. 'See you.'

'Have a good weekend,' nodded Mrs Ludwig, already forgetting her.

Kit went home on the underground. It was crowded on this wet winter night. The train smelled of wet mackintosh and too many people crowded together. But the crowds were cheerful. Everybody partied on a Friday night, after all.

Except me, thought Kit, getting out at Notting Hill and turning north, into the Palladian jungle. She thought it with relief.

There had been a time when she partied every night, desperate to keep up with the in-crowd. It had cost her a degree, her self-respect and, very nearly, her health. These days she was very glad to be a non-party-goer.

Fridays were the nights Kit washed her hair and listened to opera. She had done piano concertos and given up on them without regret. But she still had hopes of coming to like opera.

So much to learn, she thought. So much to experience. Who needed to date?

She ran up the steps of a white stucco terrace house and let herself in. The terrace was elegantly proportioned but, once inside, the house was all homely chaos. Tonight it smelled of joss-sticks and an ominous citrus and cinnamon mix that meant her landlady was brewing punch.

Kit lived in the basement flat, courtesy of her brother-in-law, whose aunt owned the house. She was an ex-ballerina and full of artistic temperament. It was Tatiana who was responsible for the chaos. Tatiana, too, who burned joss-sticks and threw wild parties on a Friday night.

Kit tiptoed past the door to Tatiana's part of the house. Her landlady was quite likely to demand her presence at tonight's bash if she caught her. She thoroughly disapproved of Kit's antisocial tendencies.

'Get a life,' she had said as they passed on the front steps only that morning. Kit was coming back from her early swim. 'The only things you do outside this flat are work and swim.'

'I'm taking driving lessons,' Kit had said defensively.

Tatiana snorted. 'You need to get your hands on a man, not a combustion engine,' she snapped.

'Been there. Done that,' said Kit flippantly.

But Tatiana looked up at her like a wise old tortoise. 'Oh, yes? When?'

Kit shook her head, half annoyed, half amused in spite of herself. 'Why do you keep on about it? It's like living with the thought police!'

Tatiana was not offended. Indeed, she looked rather pleased.

A suspicion occurred to Kit. 'Has Lisa put you up to this?'

Tatiana sniffed. 'She didn't have to. It's not natural. You only go out if you've got an evening class. A girl your age ought to be having fun.'

'Dating,' interpreted Kit with a resigned sigh.

'Having fun,' corrected Tatiana. 'Especially a girl who looks like you.'

Kit flinched.

'Golden hair and green eyes,' said Tatiana rancorously. 'And you move like a dancer. You could be stunning if you wanted. Only you dress in potato sacks. And you never go anywhere.'

'I go where I want,' said Kit, losing her rag. 'And wear what I want. If you can't take it, I can always move out.'

But Tatiana had backed away from the challenge. She had flung up her hands and retreated into her flat, muttering in Russian.

Kit grinned to herself now, recalling it. She did not often win a battle of wills with her landlady. Still, no point in inviting a rematch, she thought, edging down the stairs to her own flat as softly as she knew how.

She heard the phone ringing even before she had the key in the lock. She flung the door open and dived on it, before the ringing could bring Tatiana out of her lair.

'Hello? Kit?'

'*Lisa?*' said Kit incredulously. Her sister was supposed to be in a tropical paradise, holidaying with her naturalist husband while she recuperated from a series of winter infections. 'What on earth are you doing ringing me? You're supposed to be relaxing on a palm-fringed beach.' And then, quickly, 'There's nothing wrong with Nikolai, is there?'

'I wouldn't know. I hardly see him.' Lisa's voice sounded as if she were at the bottom of the ocean. It did nothing to disguise the waspish tone.

'Oh,' said Kit, feeling helpless.

'He told me the hotel was hosting a conference about local conservation and he might look in. I thought he meant he was going to go to a couple of talks. But he's there all the time. And now he's agreed to speak.'

Kit knew Lisa. From the sound of it, her sister could hardly contain her rage.

'And the damned hotel is empty except for men at conferences. What genius ever went and built a super de luxe hotel on the edge of a war zone? I ask you!'

'War zone?' repeated Kit, alarmed.

Lisa sounded impatient. 'Seems to have died down at the moment. That's the reason for all the conferences, I gather. But no one in their right mind would come here for a *holiday*.'

Kit looked at her dark window onto the lavish communal gardens that the terrace shared. The rain lashed at it.

'If you've got sunshine, you've got a holiday,' she said firmly. 'You don't even want to think about what London is like tonight.'

Lisa said rapidly, 'Then come and share it with me.'

'What?'

'Why not? Come and keep me company.'

'Oh, come on, Lisa. I've never liked playing gooseberry.'

Lisa gave a hard laugh. 'You wouldn't. I never see Nikolai. That's the trouble. There's nobody to talk to. And damn-all to do.'

Kit kicked off her shoes and curled her legs under her. She stuck the telephone under her ear and leaned forward to turn on the fire.

'Hey, hang on. It can't be that bad. No grey skies. No puddles. And you've got leaves on the trees. Who needs anything to do when they can laze on a beach?'

There was a pause. Not a comfortable pause.

What on earth had happened? thought Kit. The last she had heard, Lisa and Nikolai could not wait to get away together. Lisa had had a series of mysterious viruses in the weeks running up to Christmas. They had left her weak and wan and uncharacteristically tearful. And Nikolai had been continent-hopping most of the year. This tropical holiday was supposed to get them some quality time together.

Now only four days into the holiday, Lisa could hardly speak her husband's name without spitting.

'Anyway, holidays in a tropical paradise are not in my budget,' said Kit into the silence. There was a hint of desperation in her voice. 'I can't afford it.'

'I can.'

There was no doubt about that. Lisa was head of trading in a London bond-dealing room. Her annual bonus alone made Kit's eyes water.

But she still said, 'You've done enough for me over the years, Lisa. I'll pay my own way now that I can.'

'But you can't afford a tropical holiday and I—need you here,' Lisa added, so softly Kit could hardly hear her. 'I really need some support, Kit.'

Oh, lord, thought Kit, startled. What's going on here? She had never heard Lisa say she needed support in the whole of her fast-paced life.

'Come and keep me company, Kit.' Her voice was tight. Kit knew that note. It meant Lisa was determined not to cry. And then, the controlled voice cracking, 'I'm so *lonely*.'

Kit was too shocked to say anything.

'There's a flight on Sunday. I've booked you on it provisionally. At least think about it.'

She rang off without saying goodbye.

Kit paced the room, disturbed.

Had Lisa and Nikolai fallen out? But why? Lisa's husband was an aristocrat and the Romaine sisters came from the wrong side of the tracks. A long way on the wrong side of the tracks, as Lisa had once told him.

Lisa had got her education and her high-profile job entirely by her own efforts. Yet that had never seemed to be a problem before. If she'd been asked, Kit would have said Count Nikolai Ivanov was more in love with his raggle-taggle wife now than he had had been when he married her.

But on the phone just now Lisa hadn't sounded like a loved wife. And Kit loved Lisa. She was more than a sister. She was Kit's best friend.

Maybe this was the time to sink her principles, after all.

She was still wavering when there came a tap on the French window.

Tatiana, thought Kit. Normally she and her landlady had a slightly edgy relationship. Tatiana thought Kit was boring at best; at worst, a passenger clinging to her successful sister's coat tails. Kit thought Tatiana was an eighty-year-old delinquent. But they met on their affection for Lisa.

So Kit opened the door with unusual enthusiasm.

'Lisa has spoken to you,' said Tatiana, recognising the enthusiasm and diagnosing its source with accuracy.

'Yes. I'm worried.'

'So am I,' admitted Tatiana.

To Kit's astonishment she sat on the sofa and made herself comfortable without once complaining about Kit's pale cushions. Tatiana liked her furnishings *bright*.

'She sounded wretched,' said Kit, biting her lip.

'When did you talk to her?'

'Just now. She wants me to go out there.'

Kit waited for Tatiana to say, Don't interfere. Tatiana thought the only person who was allowed to interfere in the affairs of Lisa and Nikolai was herself. But she didn't.

The vivid, lined face creased into an expression of profound foreboding.

'You talked to her *now*?'

Kit nodded. 'I just put the phone down on her. Or rather she put the phone down on me. She sounded really upset.'

Tatiana's monkey face looked as if she was about to burst into tears. 'Do you know what the time difference is?'

Kit was bewildered. 'What's that got to do with anything?'

'It's seven o' clock here. That makes it three in the morning at Coral Cove,' said well-travelled Tatiana Ivanova. '*Three*. And she's calling you. Where's her husband, for goodness' sake?'

Kit stopped her pacing, shocked.

'No wonder she sounded so—fragile,' she said, almost to herself.

'You'd better go,' said Tatiana. Adding, with that practicality that Kit always found so disconcerting, all mixed up with the crystal-balls philosophy and the joss-sticks, 'Do you need some cash?'

Kit shook her head. 'Lisa's booked me a ticket and paid for it. And I haven't used my credit card for anything this month. I'll be fine.'

'You'll need a tropical wardrobe,' said Tatiana, who thought clothes were the window of the soul.

Kit shrugged.

Tatiana bounced off the sofa. 'You are impossible. Look at you. Wonderful golden hair, wonderful skin, pretty face. You're tall and as slim as a model. Why on earth aren't you out there buying disgracefully short skirts and giving everyone a heart attack with your skin-tight tops?'

Like Lisa.

Neither of them said it. They both knew what Tatiana meant.

Kit said more sharply than she meant, 'Just stop it, Tatiana. I dress the way I like.'

Tatiana brooded. 'Well, at least get yourself a swimsuit. I saw some pretty bikinis in—'

Kit went rigid. 'No bikinis,' she almost shouted.

Tatiana stared.

'I'll get a one-piece from the sports shop,' Kit said in a more moderate tone.

'And some shorts. And light tops. You have no idea how hot it's going to be,' Tatiana warned her. 'Something respectable to wear in the evening. Oh, and a straw hat to keep your head covered in the sun. Coral Cove is on the Equator.

You have to be careful. Blondes more than most.'

'Thank you for the advice. But won't I be able to buy straw hats and stuff there?'

Tatiana snorted. 'This is not a teen beach club, you know. There won't be hot-dog stands and market traders. Nikolai said Coral Cove was one of the most sophisticated hotel complexes in the world.'

Kit narrowed her eyes at her. 'So?'

Tatiana was unimpressed by the dangerous glint. 'You'll feel out of place if you don't dress properly,' she warned impressively.

'Well, it's an empty sophisticated hotel complex at the moment,' said Kit, refusing to be impressed.

'All the more reason to keep up the proper standards.'

'Tough toenails. I don't suppose I meet their standards in the first place.'

Tatiana sighed. 'You have such a chip on your shoulder, Kit.'

'Only when I'm around people who rabbit on about proper standards,' said Kit dangerously.

Tatiana gave up. She turned to go.

The French window swung gently. An elegant white paw, like an arm in a long evening glove, appeared round it.

'That cat,' said Tatiana with disfavour.

Kit chirruped at it. The paw pointed daintily and was followed by the rest of the animal. A small brindled cat oozed round the door and leapt for the rug in front of the fire. It began to wash itself rapidly. Kit smiled.

'Cats,' muttered Tatiana. 'Anyone would think you were a hundred, not twenty-two.'

'She's only visiting.'

Tatiana cast her kohl-rimmed eyes to heaven. 'You ought to be having visitors who are tall, dark and handsome and make you rethink your position on bikinis.'

Kit shook her head, impatient. 'Oh, not that again. Why does it matter to you what I do with my life?'

'Because you've only got one,' said Tatiana forcefully. 'And I can't bear waste.'

There was a fraught silence. Kit was the first to look away. She bit her lip.

Tatiana did not know the horrors that sometimes rode Kit, when the nights were long and she couldn't sleep. Even Lisa did not know all of them. But Kit had some very good reasons for her position on bikinis. And tall and handsome visitors were definitely not welcome.

She said with difficulty, 'Look, I know this doesn't fit in with your world view, Tatiana. But not all of us are brave enough to go everywhere and experience everything.'

'Bravery has nothing to do with it.'

'Oh, yes, it does,' said Kit quietly. She faced her simmering landlady squarely. 'Believe me, I do the best I can. But I've done the tall, dark and handsome visitor bit, years ago. Didn't work. In my experience men just tear your heart out. And, when they've finished that, they mess with your head. I'm not brave enough to go through it all again. And that's the honest truth.'

Tatiana was silent for a moment. Then she nodded sadly. 'All right. It's your life. So it's your business. But you'll go to Coral Cove?'

Kit nodded. 'I'll go.'

Lisa was waiting at the small airport. Kit thought she would break, Lisa hugged her so convulsively.

'You came. God bless you, Kit. Was it difficult to get time off?'

Kit grinned. 'On the contrary. The clients fell on my neck when they heard they'd got another week to clear the house before I move in with the industrial cleaning machinery. I'm their favourite person.'

Lisa heaved her roll-bag over one shoulder and linked arms with her.

'I'm really grateful, honest,' she said soberly. 'I know it was a lot to ask.'

'Oh, yeah, really tough. A whole week at your expense on a private tropical island with cordon-bleu cooking. Only a genuine saint would sign up for that one,' said Kit drily.

Lisa sighed. 'Well, it's not as great as it sounds. The gardens are pretty and the sea is warm. And, when you've said that, you've said everything. I hope you've brought plenty to read.'

Kit looked at her ironically. Lisa laughed.

'Yes, of course you have. What is it this month? Russian?'

'War poems. But I've brought some paperbacks as well,' Kit said reassuringly.

'Thank God for that. I've read all mine.'

Lisa led the way out into a blazing heat so strong that Kit gagged. She put up a hand to shade her suddenly dazzled eyes. Lisa sent her a quick, remorseful look.

'I hope you brought sunglasses. I didn't think to tell you.'

'Neither did Tatiana,' said Kit ruefully. 'Though she made me bring a cocktail dress.'

Lisa stared. 'A cocktail dress? You?'

'She's very strong-minded when she gets going.'

Lisa gave a crack of laughter. 'I remember.' She hugged Kit. 'Oh, it's so great to see you. We'll get you some shades and the local insect repellent and then we're on our way. A new experience for you—you get to ride in a helicopter.'

Coral Cove took Kit's breath away. It sat in the sunlit ocean like a toy island. But as the helicopter came in over the land she made out huge trees, great gashes in the forest cover where rivers had carved their way in their path to the sea, and even— She leaned forward, entranced.

'Is that a waterfall?'

'Probably,' said Lisa, unexcited. 'Nikolai and I have got a little one just above our cottage. There's quite a big one about half an hour's walk from the main hotel garden. We'll go up there this evening, if you like.'

Kit sat back in her seat with a sigh of perfect pleasure.

'Sun, sea *and* waterfalls,' she said blissfully. 'I forgive Tatiana for the cocktail dress. I forgive Tatiana for *everything*.'

But that evening they did not walk to the waterfall. That evening Lisa was locked in her room not speaking to anyone. And Nikolai, having welcomed Kit through gritted teeth, had gone back to his conservationists.

Kit looked into the ferociously formal dining room, thought of the little black and silver number that Tatiana had thrust into her bag, and decided that she would pass on dinner. On the other hand, while everyone else was dining she might be able to swim undisturbed in the delectable lagoon she and Lisa had explored earlier.

'They have swimming stuff if you haven't brought anything to swim in,' had said Lisa, who knew her sister very well.

'No. I have.' It was not a bikini, in spite of Tatiana's best efforts, but it would be just fine for swimming.

Kit had been terribly tempted. The water was turquoise. Little wavelets stirred but the sand bars held back ocean-sized waves. It had looked like heaven—except that there were three other people already swimming there. Kit did not take her clothes off in front of anyone, not even to swim.

'Maybe later,' Lisa had said with understanding.

And now, thought Kit, looking at the rapidly darkening sky over the lagoon, later had come. Everyone was eating, or getting ready to eat, or still locked in their conference. She could swim safe from fear of disturbance. It was irresistible.

She went back to her cottage and climbed into the one-piece swimsuit she had picked up at the charity shop. Then she pulled on an ankle-length cotton robe and went to plunge into her first tropical sea.

*   *   *

Philip Hardesty's eyes drifted back towards the great open windows yet again.

Someone was swimming in the lagoon. From his seat on the podium, Philip could see the swirl of phosphorescence. The lone figure cut through the undifferentiated blackness of night sky and water with arc after arc of shooting stars.

It looked wonderful, he thought. Cool and airy and—wonderful.

His shirt seemed to be sticking to him. Unobtrusively—or at least he hoped it was un-obtrusive—he ran a finger round the inside of his collar. If only he could loosen his tie.

The hotel conference room was unbearably hot. Even with the old-fashioned ceiling fans twirling at full speed, and all windows onto the terrace flung wide open, the air seemed to hover like a storm cloud. Of course, the television lights did not help, he thought fairly. He was always fair. It was his profession.

Just at the moment his profession required him to sit behind this array of microphones, telling half-truths in the hope that people believed them sufficiently to stop killing each other. So he dragged his gaze back from the lone swimmer and nodded courteously to the next journalist.

'Your question, Herr Dunkel?'

He knew the man. He had faced him at Press briefings like this in three separate countries in the last year alone. His question was a good one. A German, the man had twenty years more experience than Philip.

But then, everyone in this room probably has more experience than I have, Philip thought. And I'm so *tired*.

For a moment his confidence faltered. But then he pulled himself together. Everyone was looking at him. If he didn't have confidence in the peace negotiation that he was just putting in motion, who would?

And Dunkel's question deserved an answer.

Philip took a moment to consider. Then answered swiftly and fluently, as he always did.

Beyond the French windows, the lagoon stretched and sighed. It beckoned him like a playful animal. Or a dark angel.

Philip ignored it and took another question.

And another. And another.

Until at last the Press conference was over and his local minder was steering him towards the banquet.

The next performance, thought Philip. More diplomacy disguising desperation, more half-truths. More hope against hope. More anger behind the smiles. More pretence. He felt deathly tired.

'Give me a moment,' he said to his minder, with that gentle courtesy that never faltered, no matter how many people were losing their tempers at the negotiating table. 'I'd like a breath of air.'

The man switched stride. Philip stopped him.

'Alone, if you wouldn't mind.'

The man gave him a wide grin full of gold teeth, and nodded.

'Bar is over that way,' he said helpfully.

He gestured away from the lagoon towards a great circular swimming pool. It was floodlit and there was a thatched bar beside it. Philip thanked him. But he did not look at the well-illuminated path to the pool. Instead he looked longingly out to sea.

He nodded to the man and stepped through the French windows.

At once the tropical night embraced him. The air was hot and sweet, heavy with the scent of trumpet vines. He breathed it in, luxuriating.

Philip glanced up. The swathe of silent stars shimmered. There were millions of them, frosted droplets suspended from a gigantic spiral. He could see the sky turning…turning… He shut his eyes, dazzled.

In the big reception room behind him everyone was talking. It reverberated like a drum. Philip winced and opened his eyes.

I must get away, he thought urgently. Even five minutes would make all the difference.

A pebble-edged pathway skirted the gardens and led out to a sand bar that curved round the lagoon. He took it, walking quickly. The sounds of the busy hotel receded.

At the junction with the sand bar, he stopped and listened: cicadas, falling fruits, the soft lull of the water and his own breathing. No voices; no *demands*. He let out a long, savouring breath.

The lone swimmer was still out on the reef. Only now she was diving, her body curving into a pure arc before straightening to enter the water, taut as an arrow. Luminescence exploded around her. She bobbed up to the surface and pushed back her sopping hair.

Obviously she thought she was alone. She waved her arms above her head, laughing aloud. Then, quick and supple as an otter, she tumbled into a couple of mischievous somersaults. They set up a sparkling wheel of phosphorescence for a fraction of a second.

The whole picture was physical delight incarnate. Philip realised he was smiling.

He looked back at the hotel. He had to go back; the banquet was just another stage in the peace negotiations. He had to chair it, just as he had chaired the meeting for the last three days. Just as he would chair the next week's round upon round of talks.

But the girl's uninhibited game in the water reminded him that it was a long time since he had done anything for the sheer joy of doing it.

He turned his back on the talk and the banquet and went out along the palm-fringed spur of impacted sand. It curved round the lagoon like an embracing arm. As he walked he could see the stardust trail that the swimmer was making above the water. She was streaking back to land. They would reach the end of the sand bar at the same time.

Just five minutes, he promised himself.

The girl got there first. She must have heard his approach. She trod water, turning towards the sound.

'Who's there?' Her voice was husky, hurried, a little alarmed. 'Lisa?'

It was not fair to alarm her, just for the pleasure of watching her carefree play in the water. And he was, he reminded himself with faint bitterness, always fair. Wasn't he?

Suppressing his reluctance, Philip stepped out of the shadow of the palm trees. 'No.'

She drew a little startled breath. He supposed she would be justified in being fearful at the sudden appearance of a solitary stranger. This hotel was on the edge of a war zone, after all, for all its international luxury.

He said in his calmest voice, 'Don't be afraid. I'm staying here. Just taking a walk before dinner.'

'Oh.'

The calm tone worked its usual magic. Her alarm appeared to subside. She trod water, her head on one side.

'Are you a naturalist?'

Philip hesitated. It was a long time since he had been with anyone who didn't know exactly who he was, why he was here and what his attitude was going to be to any subject that might be raised. Now he realised that he would relish anonymity, however brief. He didn't answer her question.

She swam towards him. Her languorous strokes set up sparkling fireworks in the water. He went onto one knee and leaned down to stir the lagoon as it lapped softly against the sand bar. It glittered, swirling.

The girl reached him. She looked down at the underwater sparklers, laughing.

'Crazy, isn't it? I don't know what makes it do that.'

'Bio-luminescence,' said Philip.

She stood up. The water reached her waist, rocking gently. She moved with it, seeming wholly at one with the water.

'What?'

'Micro-crustacea. They give off light the way fireflies do on land.'

'Really?' She was polite but not quite certain that he knew what he was talking about.

Philip grinned unseen and decided to pull the stops out to impress her.

'Unless they're euphausiacea. In that case they have built-in searchlights,' he told her, deadpan.

She was not easy to impress.

'Are you laughing at me?'

Good girl, thought Philip, surprising himself.

'No. You can look it up. Try eucarida in the encyclopaedia and work from there.'

He could see that she would do exactly that.

'Eucarida,' she said, committing it to memory. 'How do you know that? Are you here with the conservation group?'

Conservation group? Philip hesitated. He vaguely remembered the security report on the other groups in the hotel. Now he thought about it, he was not surprised. This was an area that was rich in uncodified species as well as wild men and wars.

'No,' he said regretfully, 'I'm not with the conservation group. But once—a hundred years ago—I thought I might be a marine biologist.'

She tilted her head in the darkness. It was a perfect shape, under the long mermaid's hair that curved onto her shoulders. Her shadowed body looked as if it had turned smooth and streamlined in the sea, so that was the element to which it now naturally belonged. He had a sudden almost overwhelming longing to run his hand down that smooth curve from the crown of her head to her unseen toes.

But she was saying, amused, 'A hundred years ago? You don't sound that old.'

Philip was disconcerted. In spite of the darkness—or maybe because of it—she seemed to sense it. She laughed again and began to dance a little in the water.

'You're *not* that old, are you?' she teased.

She had a husky voice with a slight catch in it, as if she was constantly on the brink of tears or laughter. It fascinated him.

'What makes you say that?' he parried, wanting to keep her talking. Even though she could not see him, he smiled at the beguiling shadow.

'Well, if you were, you wouldn't be standing here talking to me, wishing you were in the water too,' she said softly.

This time he was more than disconcerted. He was struck to the heart. He had not known he was wishing any such thing. But he was. He *was*.

Philip's smile died.

I can't afford this, he thought.

The girl did not pick up his turmoil. She did a little boogie on the spot. Those unseen toes were deliberately stirring a thousand shooting stars into zipping through the turbulent water.

'Come on in. It's lovely and warm.'

Oh, but he was tempted. He could not remember ever being so tempted before. To slip out of the grey suit, the tie and the good manners and slide into the water with her. To swim and play like seals. Not responsible to anyone. Not responsible *for* anyone. Just abandoning himself to the moment and the lovely, uncomplicated girl.

He was already discarding the lightweight grey jacket, standard garb for negotiators in tropical climates, when she put both hands on the sand bar and lifted herself out of the water. The water streamed off her in an unearthly glow. Long legs, long hair, limbs that were supple and warm and headily female. Philip's body responded instantly and unequivocally.

She was unaware of that too.

'They leave the swimming stuff in a hut under the trees.'

'Do they?' His voice sounded odd even to himself.

'Yes, it's amazing. Like a tree house only on the ground. There were a lot of sky-blue birds with tails like saloon dancers' skirts zipping around it earlier.'

'The Asian fairy bluebird,' said Philip, in his most detached tone. His palms were wet. He

Hardly realising what he was doing, he pulled her towards him.

He heard her startled breath. He felt smooth shoulders and the damp stuff of her swimsuit over the glorious warmth of breast and hip. He felt bone and muscle and curving flesh. Even then, he might have stepped away.

But then he felt her response.

For a tiny second she was his, mouth to fierce mouth.

Then, like water, she slid out of his arms and dived back into the lagoon, powering away for the open sea.

Behind him, there were voices.

'Sir Philip? Are you there?' The minder, slightly ruffled, as if someone had taken him to task.

'Are you all right, sir?' That was his aide. Presumably the one doing the taking to task.

And the restaurant manager. 'Can we seat the guests now, sir? We can start to serve the meal as soon as you like.'

Responsibility! Here it comes again, thought Philip. *Back in the cockpit and off we go for another trip round the same old sticking points.*

But they were his sticking points. And his responsibility.

He turned and went to do his duty.

But he sent a last, lingering glance after the silver trail flickering away from him, never to return.

CHAPTER TWO

KIT powered through the water until she got out to the open sea. She knew she had passed the last sand bar because the water was cooler and the waves had begun to slap against her face.

She stopped and trod water, looking back. She was startled to find how far she had come without realising it.

'Life is just one new experience after the other,' she muttered with irony.

She paddled herself round to face the bay.

The main hotel building was brilliant with lights. Stretched out along the shoreline there were little pockets of illumination. Mentally Kit traced the map of the island: beach barbecue; swimming pool; bower bar; wedding temple. Higher up the cliffs, there were the individual lights of the guest cottages themselves. Paths up to the cottages were lit by pale stretches of party lights, hanging in swathes from tree to tree. They looked like diamond necklaces pinned out against green velvet.

It looked pretty and welcoming and safe.

Safe, Kit told herself. *New experiences, fine. But basically I'm safe.*

The tall stranger had laid hands on her. OK. But he had not grabbed. He had not held her with the terrible force that made her feel she could not breathe. And he had let her go without a moment's hesitation when she pulled away.

And she had touched him first.

That was the newest experience of all. Kit had not let any man touch her since Johnny had held her and shaken her, shouting at her that he did not love her; he never had. And tonight—

She drew a shaky breath. It brought too much salt water with it. Kit flapped her arms, coughing.

Oh, the stranger had kissed her, sure. But hadn't she kissed him back?

She cleared her throat and drew several deep, recovering breaths. She had to work hard to stay upright against the waves.

Oh, yes, she had kissed him back. How long since that had happened? She had clung to Johnny like a thing possessed. But when he kissed her, all she had been aware of was terror that, if she did not put on a good show of arousal, he would leave her.

Which of course he did, in the end. Kit shivered.

A breeze riffled the water. In spite of the warmth of the night, she felt goose bumps rise on her shoulders where they were exposed to the air. This was not the time to think about Johnny. It was time she was getting back.

She began to swim to the shore, suddenly recognising how tired she was. Swimming in the municipal pool did not prepare you for this, thought Kit. She conserved her energy and concentrated on maintaining a steady stroke.

By the time she got there, her arms were shaking with tiredness and she could hardly move her legs any more. It did not stop her looking for the stranger. Or being disappointed when she saw that he had gone.

'Just as well,' Kit told herself grimly. 'Enough new experiences already.'

But she could not curb a faint feeling of frustration as she squelched along to the swimming hut to retrieve her clothes.

She did not tell Lisa. Neither what had happened nor what—more startlingly—she wished had happened.

Kit was not sure why she kept her own counsel. Normally she told Lisa everything. Well, nearly everything. Not about Johnny. Not about the other, unbearable, thing. But everything else. She had had to keep secrets from her anxious mother. But Lisa knew all that there was to know—or at least all that Kit could bear to tell.

But tonight she was not even tempted to confide. Maybe because Lisa showed no interest at all in how she had spent her solitary evening.

In fact, Lisa was monosyllabic. Kit had showered and changed in her luxury cottage, then wandered up the cliff to say goodnight to her sister and brother-in-law before taking her jet lag to bed.

But there was no sign of Nikolai. Lisa was sitting alone in the dark on the little terrace outside her cottage. In fact, Kit nearly did not see her. If it were not for the squeak of the rattan rocking chair, she would have thought the cottage was deserted.

'Lisa?' said Kit tentatively into the murmurous night.

At first she thought Lisa must have fallen asleep. Or was not going to answer for some reason. She was even on the point of turning away.

And then Lisa said, 'All right, you've got me.' She sounded weary. 'You'd better come up.'

There were spiral steps from the pathway up to the terrace. Kit went up them carefully. She was halfway up when a match scraped and Lisa appeared at the top, carrying a storm lantern. One look at her face and Kit ran the rest of the way.

'What is it?' she said involuntarily.

Lisa had been crying. No doubt of it. Even in the uncertain light of the oil lamp, her eyes were swollen.

Lisa folded her lips together. 'Not feeling too well. Sorry.'

Kit looked at her narrowly. Lisa was never ill. Or she never had been until this winter.

Lisa looked away. 'How's your cottage?' she said with a palpable effort.

'Very luxurious. Lisa, what's wrong?'

'Nothing.'

'Where's Nikolai?'

Lisa shrugged. 'Having a drink with other boffins, I suppose.'

Kit was concerned. 'Why didn't you go too? Not because you were waiting for me?'

Lisa shook her head. 'Didn't feel like it.'

Kit's concern grew. 'But surely, Nikolai must have wanted you with him.'

'Who knows what Nikolai wants?' said Lisa with sudden bitterness. 'Oh, forget it! Tell me how you like your cottage. Found out how the fans work yet?'

Kit gave up. Lisa would tell her what was going on in her own good time if she wanted to.

So she said cheerfully, 'Yup. Sussed the fans. Sussed the electric blinds. Got rid of the television and the mirrors.'

Lisa gave a rather forced laugh. 'You and your anti-mirror campaign!'

Kit grinned. 'I've been beaten by the one in the bathroom. It's fixed to the wall.'

Lisa managed a better laugh this time.

'Anyway, if it weren't for all the drawer lining paper with wedding bells on, I'd really feel at home now.'

Her attempt at a joke was partly rewarded. Lisa threw back her head and laughed uninhibitedly.

'Oh, they do like their wedding bells,' she agreed. 'They're quite convinced people will start getting married here again as long as they don't admit that they ever had a reason to stop. Have you seen their brochures? You can't go on a fishing trip without it being called a honeymoon cruise!'

Kit pulled a comical face. 'Even the basket of shampoo and stuff in the bathroom has got a gift tag in it. *For the Bride*,' she said in disgust. 'It feels as if I'm here under false pretences.'

Lisa's smile died.

'You and me both.'

There was a nasty silence. Kit waited for her sister to retract—or confide what was wrong. She did neither.

Instead she got up and went to the balustrade. She stood there scanning the horizon. She had obviously bought a native sarong locally. It stirred gently in the sea breeze.

'It should be the ideal place for a honeymoon,' she said almost to herself.

'Or a love affair,' said Kit. She was not quite sure why she said it. 'My cottage is as near isolated as you can get and still be fifteen minutes' walk from breakfast. A classic lovers' hideaway.' Her voice sounded odd, even to her own ears.

Lisa seemed to notice that at last. She turned, looking at Kit with sudden concern.

'Are you all right with that? I didn't think. You're not jumpy about being on your own?'

'I'm jumpy about being in a room full of strangers,' Kit said drily. 'On my own I can handle.'

'Because you could always sleep here if you are,' said Lisa, not attending. 'Unhappy about being alone, I mean.'

Kit shook her head in undisguised horror. She could see where this was going. It had to be stopped—and soon.

'Look,' she said frankly, 'I said I didn't want to be a gooseberry. Well, I don't want to be a buffer zone either. You and Nikolai have your problems, you sort them out on your own.'

Lisa did not answer for a moment. Then she said in a low voice, 'You're right. Sorry, Kit, I shouldn't have tried to involve you.'

'What *is* it with you two?' said Kit, torn between exasperation and sisterly sympathy.

But Lisa made a little gesture, silencing her. And soon after she said she was tired and wanted to go to bed.

So Kit wandered back to her cottage on her own. The cottage that she'd said herself was a dream of a lovers' hideaway.

She gave a little superstitious shudder as she remembered that. What on earth had made her think of that, much less say it?

'You're suffering from evening-class withdrawal,' she muttered to herself bracingly.

But really it was not something she found easy to laugh about. In the privacy of the scented night she could almost—*almost*—imagine it.

If she half closed her eyes she could pretend that there was a man walking beside her. She knew he was tall but his features were shadowy. She knew his voice, though. It was a deep voice that seemed to reach through to the core of her.

Her lips parted. She knew that voice all right. It was so calm, so controlled. And beneath the control? Kit's breath came faster.

He had been so cool with his talk of wildlife. So removed from the allure of the night when his busy companions had called him back into the bright hotel rooms. But the mouth on hers had been fiery hot. And he had not found it easy to let her go.

What am I thinking? Have I cast him in the role of my lover, then? Kit stopped dead, shaken. Even though it was only in her imagination, she did not like it. She knew just how dangerous imaginings like that could be. She fought for common sense.

'If you have exciting dreams tonight, you have no one but yourself to blame,' Kit told herself with irony. 'You've got to get a hold on that imagination. You can't go to pieces because you're in a tropical paradise.'

Paradise was just about it. The night was full of noises. Birds squawked. She wondered if they were the iridescent blue ones she had seen earlier. What had the tall stranger said they were called? Fairy bluebirds?

'Never mind paradise. This is turning into Fantasy Island,' Kit told herself crisply. 'Get a grip, for heaven's sake.'

But it was not easy when insects chirruped a lullaby. Leaves rustled. But Kit had told Lisa the truth: she was not afraid of the sound of nature or of her own company. It was people—their demands and then their careless, unthinking cruelty—that frightened her.

And yet she had kissed that man as if she was not frightened at all.

'I must have been out of my mind,' Kit muttered.

Her body gave a little remembering shiver of delight that told her she still was.

Jet lag or not, it was a long time before she got to sleep.

The banquet was interminable. Philip was sitting next to the development minister. The minister had been at university in Michigan and was full of cheerful stories.

Philip tried to concentrate. He really did. But his mind kept slipping sideways to the girl. Her husky voice. Her seal-smooth body. Her sheer joy in the water.

Her mouth under his.

He shifted in his seat and found the minister was laughing expectantly. He clearly wanted Philip to agree with something he had just said. Long experience had taught Philip how dangerous even a noncommittal nod could be. He really had to get a handle on this evening.

He said with his usual gentleness, 'I'm sorry, Minister. I missed that.'

The minister sobered. There was something oddly intimidating about that quiet courtesy.

He forgot the joke he had been telling. He said sharply, 'You do realise this is all useless?

Without Rafek, no agreement will be worth the paper it's written on.'

To the minister's fury, Philip nodded as if he had just made a brave stab at a crossword clue.

'Good point.'

'Well, what are you going to do about it?' said the minister belligerently.

Philip gave him one of his diplomatically inscrutable smiles.

The minister gave up.

But it made Philip concentrate for the rest of the evening. It was only after the toasts had been made, the compliments exchanged and the honoured delegates packed off to bed after a ceremonious goodnight that he had time to think about the girl again.

He and his team were sitting among the ruins of the banquet while hotel waiters began the process of clearing up. Philip leaned back in his chair and flexed his shoulders. The contracted muscles at the back of his neck flexed gratefully.

'Do we know who else is staying here?' he asked his personal assistant idly.

The PA knew how lucky he was to work for the youngest, most successful negotiator the UN had had in a long time. A PA's profile depended on that of his boss and Fernando was ambitious. So he did not complain that it was an unfair question. Though it was.

Instead he opened his briefcase and fished among its bulging papers.

'I gave you the list Security provided when we arrived, Philip. Do you want me to update it? Basically it's the Aid Agencies group and the conservationists, as far as I know. Journalists, of course. But not many of them are here for the duration. They'll fly back in for the final Press conference, of course.'

Philip nodded.

'So who would a tall blonde be, Fernando? Red Cross? Endangered-species lobby? Girl swims like a fish. Except, now I think of it, she didn't know about micro-crustacea.' He was talking to himself. 'So she won't be a conservationist.'

Fernando and Philip's locally appointed bodyguard exchanged glances. Fernando stopped riffling through his papers.

The bodyguard repeated the only word that made sense. 'Girl?'

'Oh, I just bumped into her,' said Philip, at his vaguest.

Neither was deceived, though their reactions were different. Fernando looked worried. And as for the bodyguard—

'You want a woman?' he said practically.

Fernando winced.

For a moment there was a glacial silence.

'I can arrange,' the bodyguard offered, cheerfully impervious.

Fernando held his breath.

Damn, thought Philip. How could he have forgotten? Chief negotiators were not supposed to have *feelings*. Appetites, yes. No matter how sordid, the system could cope with the animal urges of its delegates if it had to. Just not feelings.

He should never have mentioned the girl. He must certainly not do it again. Meanwhile he had to turn down the unwanted offer politely. The bodyguard was seconded from the local military. He could not offend him. The peace process needed all the local friends it could get in this cauldron of plots and bad faith.

'I think not,' he said at last, with icy sweetness.

Fernando let out a long, relieved breath. Philip could be crushing when he wanted. The bodyguard had not deserved a Hardesty tonguelashing.

'Cool,' he murmured in Philip's ear.

Philip acknowledged the compliment with the slightest lift of an eyebrow.

'Well, we have work to do. I'll just take a walk along the shore before I get back to it.' He stood up.

The bodyguard stood up too.

Philip shook his head. 'Alone, I think.'

But the bodyguard had been briefed at the highest levels.

'You should not walk alone, even on this island. Rafek has sympathisers everywhere. It would be a great coup for him if he kidnapped you.'

For a moment Philip rebelled. 'That's hardly likely, surely? Coral Cove is a private island.'

The bodyguard sucked his gold tooth. 'Been done before,' he said reluctantly. It clearly hurt his professional pride.

'But what about all those discreet surveillance cameras along the beach?' said Philip.

The bodyguard shrugged. 'Someone on the inside takes out a stretch of the lighting. Looks like an accident. Then Rafek's men come ashore in dinghies. They take who they want and go. No lights, no outboard motors until they're out to sea. No one knows until someone is missing from breakfast. There are just too many places to come ashore.'

He saw that Philip was frowning and misinterpreted.

'You're fine as long as you stick close to the main hotel,' he said encouragingly. 'And I'm never out of earshot.'

Philip ground his teeth silently. He could not ask about her! Now he could not even take a walk where he might bump into her! At least not without being observed. Was he to have no privacy?

But then he remembered the briefing that he too had read. To say nothing of the fierce men he had encountered in Rafek's jungle stronghold only last week. His cool professional head told him that his subordinates were right.

And just at the moment people's lives depended on him using his cool, professional head.

He nodded, reluctantly.

'All right. No solitary stroll. You can walk me back to my cabin. Then I'll work on the agenda for tomorrow. Fernando—can you let me have your minutes of that last meeting before you go to sleep?'

'Yes,' said Fernando, without resentment. He knew that Philip himself would be up long into the early hours, thinking about the issues.

Really, it was crazy that the bodyguard should have thought, even for a moment, that Philip Hardesty was looking for a woman. As long as he was working, Philip Hardesty had no time and no interest in anything but the project in hand. The man was a machine, thought Fernando, half-envious, half-repelled.

One thing was certain. Until the negotiation was successfully concluded, Philip Hardesty would not waste a second thought on any woman, thought Fernando. He waved the bodyguard away with a minatory frown and smiled reassuringly at his chief.

'I'll walk with you now, Philip. That should keep away the belly dancers.' And he gave a conspiratorial laugh.

It was written all over his assistant's face, Philip thought. He was rueful.

He thinks I'm not the sort of man to waste my time on feelings. And he's right, God help me. It was not a pleasant thought.

And then, as he went into his cottage and locked the door behind him, *I wonder if it's terminal?*

It was early when Kit first stirred. Hot dreams plucked at her. She turned restlessly, pushing the confining sheet away.

Still half-asleep, she thought she was in the sea. A sea god had come up the beach and carried her off. Not that she minded. She wanted to go. She loved the sensation of being in his arms, the power of it and the total trust. She went into the water with him, laughing.

Only now her feet were caught. They had tangled in some weed. She could not get free to follow him.

The sea god did not notice. He surged ahead of her, out to the open sea. Away. Leaving her.

'Don't go,' she called after him.

But her voice was lost in the great distance between them.

She tried again, louder. 'Don't leave me...'

And woke herself up.

Kit jerked upright, breathing hard.

She couldn't have said that. She *couldn't*. Not even in a dream. It was what she had said to Johnny. She had promised herself she would never say it again.

She made to get out of bed—and found that her legs really were trapped. She half fell out of bed and only recovered her balance by hopping on the spot.

'Typical,' muttered Kit. 'Start off tragedy. Turn to farce. Story of my life.'

Still, she felt better about the dream after that. She unwound the sheet, showered and dressed. Then she called Lisa.

Her brother-in-law answered. 'Glad you're here, Kit. Sorry I didn't manage to catch up with you again yesterday.'

'That's OK. Lisa explained you were busy.'

'Did she?' His voice was dry. 'Well, come up and have breakfast with us now. Unless you want to swim first?'

Kit looked at the sea. It was just twenty yards from her terrace and silver in the morning sun. It was wonderfully enticing. Except that there were two boats in the bay and a couple of figures running along the beach.

In theory the stranger had seen her in her swimsuit last night. But they had been in the shadows. He had not had the chance to look at her properly. The girl who did not look at herself in mirrors was not yet ready to appear in a swimsuit in front of other people, not even a couple of joggers so distant they looked like matchstick men.

'No, my swim can wait. I'll come up now.'

'Great. I'll order breakfast for three.'

But when she got there her hospitable brother-in-law was clearly on his way out after all.

One look at Lisa and Kit wished she hadn't come. It was obvious they were in the middle of a row. Lisa had her bad-tempered terrier look and Nikolai's brow was thunderous.

'Hi, Kit,' he said curtly. 'I'll see you later, Lise. This is the last day of the conference, I promise.'

Lisa shrugged her bare shoulders. Kit thought she had never seen a sarong look less alluring.

'Suit yourself. No skin off my nose.' She switched her attention to Kit ostentatiously and nodded at the breakfast set out on the terrace table. 'Mango juice?'

Kit nodded, feeling helpless.

Nikolai hesitated. Then he bent to kiss his wife. Quick as a snake, Lisa turned her head. His mouth just brushed her cheek.

He straightened. A muscle worked in his jaw. 'Tonight,' he said levelly.

Lisa did not answer that at all. She sat staring out to sea as Nikolai stamped out.

Kit's heart sank.

Lisa lost her terrier look. She leaned back in the rattan rocker and closed her eyes. For a moment Kit wondered if she really was ill. She looked very pale.

Eyes still closed, Lisa said wearily, 'That's what he says every morning. And every evening he comes back and says, ''Just one more day, Lise.'''

Kit was uncomfortable. She was in awe of her formidable brother-in-law but she liked him.

'Well, I suppose conservation *is* important.'

Lisa's laugh cracked. 'More important than his wife?' She opened her eyes. They were wet.

Wisely Kit did not attempt to answer that.

Lisa answered it herself. 'I know. I know. There is an ecological crisis here. If he thinks he has a chance to do something about it, he has to keep trying. But...'

I'm so lonely. It was what she had said to Kit on the telephone to London. She did not have to say it again. It hung in the air between them.

Kit thought suddenly: it's probably the first time she's been lonely like that in her life. She could always get any man she wanted. Maybe for once I know more than Lisa does about something.

She said slowly, 'You have to talk to him about it, you know, Lisa. Sulks won't get you anywhere.'

'*Sulks?*' Lisa was so outraged that her tears subsided. Kit saw it with relief. She did not really know what to do with a tearful Lisa. 'That's great, coming from a girl who didn't open her mouth all through my birthday party.'

'That's not fair,' protested Kit.

'Yes, it is. Every one of Nikolai's family tried to make you welcome in France. They wanted you to have a nice time. But you wouldn't swim, wouldn't ride, wouldn't even join the dancing at the end of the harvest. What was that if it wasn't sulks?'

Kit shifted her shoulders irritably. 'Well, they're grand.'

'They're my in-laws,' corrected Lisa.

'They've got titles,' muttered Kit.

Lisa sighed. 'So have I now,' she pointed out reasonably. 'I'm a countess. Are you going to stop talking to me because of it?'

'Don't be silly, of course not.'

'But you won't talk to Nikolai's grandmother because *she* is a countess too. You are such a snob.'

'I'm not. I just felt out of place at the château.'

'Oh, so you admit it now.'

'No, I don't admit anything,' said Kit with heat.

They glared at each other. After a moment, a reluctant smile dawned.

'You always did fight dirty, Lisa. All right, maybe I sulked a bit. Doesn't make any difference to what's going on here, you know. Refusing to kiss Nikolai goodbye isn't going to sort anything out.'

Lisa gave a little explosive sigh. 'When did you get to be an expert?'

Kit did not say 'When I refused to listen when Johnny wanted to talk to me'. That was an episode Lisa still did not know anything about.

Instead she said, 'What about that mango juice?'

'Oh, all right.'

Lisa poured two glasses for both of them. She flung herself back in the rattan rocker.

'I blame this place.'

'But it's beautiful,' protested Kit, startled.

Lisa's mouth tightened. 'Exactly. Beautiful and stuffed with all the trappings of happy honeymoons. It just rubs it in when you're not. Happy, I mean.'

Kit's green eyes widened. 'Oh, Lisa,' she said, her heart going out to her sister.

'Don't sympathise with me,' Lisa said dangerously. 'Tell me I ought to count my blessings. Don't let me cry, for pity's sake.'

'All right,' said Kit obediently. 'Look at the bougainvillea on the wall. It's so bright it hurts your eyes. And you've got a lovely tan. And it's going to be a gorgeous day.'

She turned her face into the soft breeze from the lagoon. It caught a few long strands of her newly washed golden hair and wafted them gently against her cheek. The breeze smelled of flowers. Kit stretched sensuously.

'And the nights. I couldn't believe it when I walked back last night. Have you ever seen such stars?'

Lisa bared her teeth. She looked ready to bite, like a blonde terrier scenting rats. It was alarming. 'Don't talk to me about the stars.'

Kit grinned, unalarmed. 'All right. What have you got against the stars?'

The terrier look went out of Lisa's pretty face. She shook her head, so that the fashionably sculpted hair flew.

'Oh, it's no fun looking at them by myself, I suppose,' she said with a flickering smile. She sighed. 'You're right, of course. Nikolai promised and— Well, I guess I'm not cut out to be the well-behaved little wife waiting while he does the important stuff.'

Kit choked. But she managed to keep a straight face. 'No,' she agreed in a strangled voice.

Lisa narrowed her eyes. 'You're laughing at me.'

'Who, me? I wouldn't dare.'

'Yes, you would.' Lisa gave a quick shrug, as if she was casting off the bad temper. She gave Kit a rueful smile. 'Quite right too. Your first time in a tropical paradise, and all I can do is spoil it by moaning! Laugh all you want.'

Kit said comfortingly, 'He said his meetings would be over today.'

'And pigs might fly. Meanwhile I've got to put up with being called the bride in Orchid Cottage,' said Lisa with feeling.

Kit laughed. 'Ah, well, I can tell you about that. I was talking to one of the gardeners yesterday. He said that this place was all set up for people to have the last word in luxury tropical weddings. Only then the war broke out. These days all the guests they get are men in suits. So every time they see a woman, they think, wow, here come the good times again.'

'Oh,' said Lisa, her ferocity dying. 'I didn't think of that. Poor things.'

Kit grinned. 'They're demoralised. They've got a bunch of economists who told them to stop the music at dinner so they could talk.'

Lisa appreciated that. She gave her old naughty smile. 'World Bank, I bet.'

Encouraged, Kit said, 'And there's some big-shot peace negotiator here who didn't even *notice* the belly dancer.'

Lisa laughed aloud at that. But then her face darkened. She said in a hard tone, 'I bet the ecology delegates wouldn't notice either. I can't tell you how long it is since Nikolai touched me.'

Ouch, thought Kit.

She dived into her mango juice. She really did not want to know about this. It was private. It was painful. And she was the last person in the world to know how to help.

But Lisa seemed to have forgotten that. Still staring out to sea, she said in a low voice, 'He doesn't want me any more, Kit.'

It was none of her business. She had always been hopeless about sex, anyway. How many times had Lisa pulled her back from the brink of disastrous relationships? That last one had nearly killed her, too.

And yet— And yet— She knew how Lisa felt.

She went over and put an arm round her competent sister.

For a moment Lisa stiffened. Then she dropped her head onto Kit's shoulder.

'I never thought it would happen to me,' she said in a stifled voice. 'I thought I could handle anything. You know?'

'You can,' said Kit stoutly.

'Not this.' Lisa detached herself from Kit's comforting arm. Her voice was flat.

Despairing, thought Kit.

She said hurriedly, 'Good sex is chemical, they say. Nothing to do with knowing someone. Or loving them. Take me, for instance—only last night I met a guy when I was swimming. We hardly spoke. But the chemistry was there all right.'

Lisa said nothing. That was unusual in itself. Normally she would have demanded all the details, delighted that Kit was showing some interest in men at last.

'Scared me a bit,' said Kit, fishing for a reaction. 'I'd forgotten that attraction could be so strong. It may be nothing more than chemistry but it certainly shakes you up.'

'Oh?' said Lisa, indifferent.

'Just goes to prove that relationships are a lot more than sex. You know me. Miss Iceberg of the century. Yet I fancied the guy like crazy and I didn't even know his name. It didn't mean anything.'

Lisa shrugged.

'Surely it works the other way round, too?' said Kit desperately. 'I mean, if you're committed to each other, you can weather a few—er—'

Lisa turned. 'Nice try, Kit. Shame it won't wash.'

'What? Why?'

'We stopped talking to each other before we stopped sleeping together,' Lisa said brutally. 'Tell me how we weather that.'

Kit gave up. There was nothing to say.

Philip ran his minder half way round the island on his morning run.

'I spent too long in the conference room yesterday. I need to get my lungs open,' he said.

He did, too. But he knew that he was really hoping to see the girl again. He didn't.

Well, it was a long shot. And if he had seen her, there wasn't anything he could do about it.

He went back to his meetings and put her out of his mind. And then, quite suddenly, he looked up from a diagram of new roads demanded by Rafek's rival guerrilla leader and—there she was!

She was running down the stepping-stone path from the cliff to the beach. He was sure it was her. This morning she was wearing cotton cut-offs and a T-shirt. Her hair was no longer plastered to her head. In fact, her hair was a true fairy-tale gold—and as long as that of any of the princesses pictured in the old books in the nursery at Ashbarrow. Philip smiled at the thought.

She was bouncing from stone to stone. The storybook hair flew out in a fan of rainbow lights as she jumped. His brain went on sifting the evidence and balancing the probabilities, as it had been taught. But his body recognised her. It was her, his water nymph of the starry night.

At last.

He had not been watching for her. Of course he hadn't. It was just chance that had him taking his coffee to the open windows every time the meeting broke for what Fernando called a comfort moment.

Who was she?

Surely she was not attached to one of the subsidiary negotiations? The delegates were all middle-aged management types. *Like me,* he thought, trying not to wince. He was thirty-five and he felt as old as the world. Whereas his golden girl was youth and spring and every playful creature he had ever seen.

For a moment he thought of the unicorn painting at Ashbarrow. It was supposed to be a study for a larger painting and the insurance was crippling because it could be an Utrillo. The unicorn was jumping through the trees, all four feet leaving the ground at once in his delight. The forest floor was scattered with daisies and anemones. They shone like jewels under the unicorn's hooves. And the feathery mane flew like the girl's gleaming hair.

How long was it since he had been to Ashbarrow? Four months? Five?

The girl would look good in his ancestral home, Philip thought idly. With her pearl-pale skin and corn-gold hair she could have been designed for the Queen's Room. All that old cherry-wood four-poster needed was a golden girl lying across its green velvet coverlet, shadowed by its cloth of gold curtains, in the lavender-scented shadows of a summer afternoon...

He brought himself up short. He was breathing a little too hard.

For a moment he could not see anything but the prism of light that fractured out of the girl's flying hair. The sea beyond her was dazzling.

He blinked and turned, intending to ask the waiter with the coffee pot who she was. He had even opened his mouth to call the man.

And a black shutter came down over his left eye. Philip went very still. Then he put his coffee down, carefully.

He looked round. No one had seen this time. Another lucky escape. That made four times that the shutter had blinded him.

It was temporary. The sight came back in a matter of minutes. But it was a complication he did not need. Everyone at the negotiations had to have total confidence in his ability to carry it through to a successful conclusion. That would not be helped by doubts over his health, however unfounded.

So he'd better stop letting himself be distracted by flying gold hair, he told himself. That was no way for a responsible peace negotiator to behave. Not even in his most private fantasies, Philip thought wryly. The girl was a distraction, no question. He could not afford distractions. And nor could all the thousands of helpless people who were expecting him to knit together some agreement between these hard-eyed men.

No more unicorns. I haven't got time for them.

So he navigated his way carefully back to the table and called the meeting to order. And, as usual, his sight cleared in a few minutes. No one noticed that there had been anything wrong.

And the chance to ask the waiter who she was had passed.

It felt, even after all these months and years of harsh discipline, like the cruellest thing he had ever denied himself.

* * *

Kit ran down to the beach without seeing anyone. She was sure-footed as a goat. She could not remember ever feeling so good. The air felt as if the sun was smiling on her while the soft sea breeze kissed her playfully.

Maybe she would put on her swimsuit and run into the sea even if those fishing boats were still out in the bay, she thought.

'Another new experience!' she told herself, grinning.

But it was impossible to hang on to her neuroses in this gorgeous place. She was surprised that Lisa had managed to resist the chance to swim from Kit's deserted beach. But Lisa had said she did not feel well again and Kit had decided not to interfere any more.

So the day was hers. And it promised to be wonderful. She was feeling brave and free and she had acres of silver sand and the sea to play in.

Just as long as she did not have to think too much about what she looked like, Kit thought. Mirrors and other people's eyes reminded her of everything she wanted to forget. But she could avoid both.

Which made it all the more odd that she had not tried to avoid the dark stranger by the lagoon last night, thought Kit, kicking up silky sand with her bare toes. What if he had followed her when she swam off?

She looked round her empty beach. The sun was as hot as a garment that someone had left by the fire. The seagulls wheeled lazily in the dazzling sky. She could smell salt and sea grasses and her own skin.

If he had followed her here to this deserted shore? Would she have been afraid then?

No, thought Kit.

She shivered slightly. Not with fear.

And at once thought, *Careful!*

That was how she had fallen into the trap last time. She had thought she was over the bad stuff. She was at college, she was enjoying her course, she had friends, plans, a life.

And then there was a *man*! Even to herself, Kit did not say she had fallen in love with Johnny. Well, not any more. It was not love, that wincing, obsessive anxiety that said she was not good enough for him. That she would never be good enough. Not for Johnny Marcus. Not for any man. Before she knew it she'd been out of her depth and spiralling all the way back into the dark place again.

Well, she had recovered. Thanks largely to Lisa, who never gave up on her. Lisa had found her the therapy group. Kit had done the rest.

Kit knew herself now. She knew the dangers. She knew how to avoid them. Mirrors were one big danger; mirrors showed her the body she recoiled from. Men who would take her out of her depth were another.

So it was just as well that the man had not followed her round to her personal beach, Kit told herself. Because when he had kissed her she had responded as she did not think she had ever responded before, not even to Johnny, and he was the leader of the pack at class.

Yet just for a second it had been there: a cameo of herself as a woman who could love and be lovable. There and gone. Between one heartbeat and the next. A small candle flame of revelation. *I can do this!*

Only then she had thought, *But I can't risk it!* and dived back into the friendly water.

But it was still there, thought Kit, stirring and stirring the sand with her toe. Even this morning. In spite of Lisa's painful confidences, in spite of all her own doubts. The tiny warmth of last night's flickering candle was still with her.

It seemed disloyal, when Lisa was so wretched. But, all on her own, Kit danced a little hop, skip and a jump in the silky sand.

He wanted me, she thought exultantly. *He really wanted me.*

CHAPTER THREE

ALL day Kit went round hugging herself secretly. She tried to laugh at herself. She knew it was silly. A stranger kissed her in the moonlight and she felt as if she was Queen of the World! It was mad. He hadn't even got a good look at her.

But he wanted me, Kit's secret self said smugly.

She somersaulted in the water with sheer delight.

Eventually the sun got too strong for her to swim, or even sit in the shade in Tatiana's sun hat and Lisa's dark glasses. So she took the map from her cottage and explored one of the coastal paths that wound up into the residual rainforest. She tried to persuade Lisa to come with her but Lisa said she wanted to read and sunbathe on her terrace. So Kit went alone.

It became the pattern for the next few days. Kit would breakfast with her sister, usually passing Nikolai on the path up to their cottage. She swam after breakfast, before the sun got too strong. Sometimes Lisa would swim with her.

Then Kit went on her solitary forest explorations and Lisa returned to her eyrie.

Kit never met anyone except an occasional hotel worker on these forays. She told herself she was not disappointed. Nikolai never appeared again, not even for dinner. Lisa's face began to look pinched.

On the fourth morning, as Kit climbed up the dew-wet hill to their cottage, she heard raised voices.

'Kit can find plenty to amuse herself with in Coral Cove. Why the hell can't you?' Her brother-in-law sounded as if he was at the end of his tether.

Lisa's voice was quiet but deadly clear. 'Maybe because Kit has lower expectations than I do.'

Oh, lord, thought Kit, and pelted up the steps to their terrace.

They were standing by the balustrade, squared up to each other like duellists.

Oh, lord!

It was going to be just like their father, thought Kit. Nikolai was going to leave Lisa. And it would break her heart!

Panic fluttered, dispelling all her pleasure in the silver morning. She could not remember their father but she had heard their mother describe the last months before he left so often, it was as if she had been part of it.

She could not bear it. She flung herself onto the terrace, saying brightly, 'Breakfast together at last. How nice.'

Nikolai said curtly, 'I'm not stopping.'

'But—'

'I've got a breakfast meeting with the UN negotiator.'

Lisa turned her shoulder and looked out to sea.

Nikolai cast her a fulminating look, then ignored her. He told Kit, 'This new guy from the UN is a real operator. The holistic approach in a big way. It looks as if we may be able to do a package deal. Peace, humanitarian aid program and conservation all rolled into one, plus the money to fund the lot. We're getting round a table this morning to compare notes.' He looked back at Lisa's stony profile. 'It's worth a shot, anyway. Isn't it?'

Lisa said nothing. Kit knew that set look.

She said desperately, 'Lisa—'

Lisa turned her shoulder.

Nikolai did not even bother to look at her again. 'So what will you do today, Kit?' he said pointedly.

Kit searched her mind desperately for something non-controversial. Inspired, she said, 'I met a man who told me about the phosphorescence.

He said it was due to—' she stumbled over the word '—eucarida. And he told me about those blue birds as well. I thought I'd rummage around on the bookshelves in the hotel lobby and see what I can find.'

Lisa gave a crack of laughter. 'See. That's all she can find to do here,' she told the sea triumphantly. 'All anyone could find to do. Some bloody zoology extension course.'

Not such an inspiration after all, thought Kit. She said hastily, 'Well, you know me. I can never pass up the chance for self-improvement.'

Neither of them laughed.

Nikolai said curtly, 'The hotel will be useless. If you're interested, you'd better look on the internet. My laptop is set up inside.'

'It is indeed,' Lisa told the ocean sweetly. 'I fall asleep to the sound of it and I wake up to the ''bing'' when he logs on.'

Kit made a face. But Nikolai was not looking at her. He was glaring at his wife's arctic profile.

'I'm sorry I've disturbed you. Maybe I'd better see if they can give me another room.'

Lisa's jaw locked. She did not look at him. 'Fine,' she said.

Nikolai looked stunned. Kit wanted to jump up and down and scream, *Don't challenge her. She never backs down from a challenge.* But they were married and if Nikolai didn't know that much about his wife, he was going to have to learn fast.

He said between tight lips, 'Fine.'

Oh, *no*, thought Kit, looking between the two of them.

Nikolai seized some papers from the table and made for the steps.

'Goodbye, Kit. Have a good day.' He ignored Lisa.

'G-goodbye,' said Kit weakly.

He ran down the steps without a backward look.

As soon as he had gone Lisa's shoulders relaxed. She spun round, blue eyes flaming.

'If he gets another room,' she announced dangerously, 'I'm on the next flight back.'

'I'm sure he won't,' said Kit soothingly. 'He's just mad. You provoked him, be fair.'

'I do not,' said Lisa unnecessarily, 'feel fair. *Men.* How right you are to have nothing to do with them.' She shook herself. 'Right. Sit down and have breakfast. Then I'll show you how to use that laptop of his.'

Kit was alarmed. 'But I'm not really used to surfing the net. I might crash it.'

Lisa gave her a sudden grin, wide and unexpected. 'How much would that cost me?'

Relieved, Kit laughed. Maybe it would work out all right after all. If Lisa could still laugh, the situation could not be hopeless.

'It's looking good,' said Philip as the room emptied that night. 'Basically we've got the jigsaw designed. Now all we've got to do is get them to talk without killing each other and we can get the deal done.'

The resident representative, a Frenchman of huge experience and reassuring cynicism, pursed his lips.

'Maybe you can bring it off, after all. I've never seen Gantalan agree to a schedule so quickly before.'

Philip smiled. 'I'd say that was because his arch rival wasn't here. Nothing to do with me. The moment Rafek turns up, both of them will have something to prove. I said it's looking good, not that we're out of the woods yet. If Gantalan and Rafek have a trial of strength, the talks could grind to a halt. Or worse.'

The Frenchman looked serious. 'You think Rafek will come, then? He never has before.'

Philip kept his expression carefully noncommittal. He had not admitted to anyone that he had had discussions with the guerrilla leader. As far as the conference knew, his uncomfortable week hiking into the rainforest was a relaxing trip looking at wildlife before the talks began.

'Who knows?' he said now evasively.

He flicked through his papers with the speed of long practice. He gave the largest pile to his assistant.

'Shred those, would you, Fernando? And make sure you get the interpreters' notebooks before they go back to their rooms and shred those too.'

The Frenchman raised his eyebrows. 'You're very thorough.'

Philip smiled. 'That's one way of putting it. I have also been called a bloody bureaucrat.'

'Haven't we all?' agreed the Frenchman drily. 'But you certainly kept the convoy moving along today.'

'The secret,' said Philip, 'is to make it plain that you will go into everything in minute detail. And you're prepared to sit there all through the night if necessary. When they start to get hungry, they get concise.'

He put the cap on his fountain pen and stowed it in the inside pocket of his jacket and picked up his folder.

The Frenchman picked up his papers more slowly.

'And what would you do if they didn't?'

'Sit as long as it takes,' said Philip coolly.

'No limit? Days? Weeks?'

'It wouldn't come to that. They have henchmen to keep under control. Wives to get back to.'

'And you don't?' said the Frenchman curiously.

He had heard a lot about Philip Hardesty on the grapevine. He was said to be an obsessive, a man without a single human emotion, a workaholic and possibly a genius. He had heard nothing at all about the workaholic's private life. Now he began to wonder if the man had one.

'No wife. No henchmen,' said Philip lightly. What was it about this place? He had never had to keep admitting it before. His solitary life had never felt so arid before, either. 'My life was bought and paid for a long time ago. I've never had to cut short a meeting in my life and everyone knows it.'

'That's quite a bargaining point,' said the Frenchman, rather taken aback.

Philip gave him his sudden engaging grin. 'I'm counting on it.'

Even more taken aback, the Frenchman found himself laughing.

'Come and have a drink,' said Philip. 'Tell me how you really think it went today—and what elephant traps are waiting for us tomorrow.'

'Thank you,' said the Frenchman, surprised by the friendliness. It did not go with the image, somehow.

'You too, Fernando,' Philip said to his aide. 'There's a bar down by the lagoon. We might avoid the trumpets and the belly dancer there.'

The Frenchman and Fernando looked at each other. They sighed. They did not particularly want to avoid the belly dancer, an imported beauty who seemed to dress entirely in mosquito netting and gold coins. But Philip was the boss. They went.

The bower bar was by the lagoon. It was lit by old-fashioned Chinese lanterns. The tables were set amid high-planted box trees for maximum privacy.

'Designed with lovers in mind,' said Lisa. Her tone was just on the hither side of sour.

She avoided a stone monkey god, playing an instrument of bells suspended from a stick, and sank into a luxuriously cushioned rattan sofa. It was set under an orange tree in a planter. The leaves moved gently in the breeze off the sea, stirring scented airs around the enclosed corner.

A place for lovers indeed, thought Kit. The sofa under the hedge was designed for a couple to hold hands and kiss without anyone else seeing them. And they were supposed to be meeting

Nikolai. He had telephoned Lisa only half an hour ago to suggest it.

'I don't really think I should be here,' Kit said uneasily. 'I'm sure he didn't mean me to come too.'

'And how long do you think he'll keep me waiting here on my own?' asked Lisa, unanswerably. 'That is, assuming he comes at all. If he gets started counting numbers of rainforest primates or something, he'll forget me altogether. I'll believe that his meetings are over when I see him. Not before.'

Kit could not put up much of an argument against that.

Lisa was wearing a pretty cotton slip dress that left her shoulders and a lot of alluring cleavage bare. Kit thought without envy that she looked even sexier than she had done when Nikolai married her. What on earth had gone wrong?

She said firmly, 'The moment he comes, I'm leaving.'

Lisa sighed. But she did not protest.

'All right. Another one of your midnight swims?'

'What do you know about my midnight swims?' said Kit suspiciously.

Lisa laughed. 'Only that the waiters approve. It's what brides are supposed to do.'

'*Brides!*'

'Well, it's what the hotel staff were all trained for, I suppose. I kind of got the impression that they appeared out of the undergrowth and scattered roses over a harem couch while you were swimming. Then melted away when you came back to shore. The two of you, that is.'

Kit shivered involuntarily. The idea was unexpectedly erotic. Kit did not usually respond to erotic ideas.

To disguise that she had done so this time, she said brightly, 'Cripes, I've had a narrow escape, haven't I?'

'I don't know.' For a moment Lisa sounded wistful and a lot younger than the Head of a Successful Trading Room had any right to sound. 'Rose petals and harem cushions might be nice.'

'Go on,' said Kit. 'Say it.' She imitated her sister. *With the right man.*

Lisa shook her head. 'I wasn't going to say that.'

'What, then?'

'If the right man wanted it,' said Lisa simply. She was not laughing any more.

Kit was shaken. 'Oh, Lise—'

Lisa held up a perfectly manicured hand in a blocking movement.

'It's all right,' she said harshly. 'Don't say anything. I don't need any more self-pity to add to the load. Get a waiter over here and let's have one of those sunset-coloured cocktails.'

Kit stood up, looking towards the bar under its pyramid umbrella of coconut matting.

'I'll go and get—'

But a waiter had materialised at the entrance to their secret bower.

'Two of the brightest cocktails you can make,' Lisa told him breezily. She was laughing again. Her social armour was back in place and locked firmly.

I wish I could do that, thought Kit. I wish I didn't broadcast my feelings loud and clear to the world. It makes me feel naked. It has always made me feel naked. Why can't I put on a decent show, like Lisa?

The waiter was certainly appreciating it. He entered into the spirit of it. In a few minutes he returned with a tall glass of liquid that went from ruby at the base to apricot at the rim and another, smaller, glass of hissing turquoise stuff.

'Tequila Sunrise, as near as dammit,' said Lisa, taking the orange one. 'But what that underwater stuff is, I haven't a clue.'

The waiter grinned. 'Not tequila. It is cane spirit and our local juices, mainly guava.'

'And the shark bait?' said Kit, looking at it dubiously.

His eyes glinted with amusement. 'Champagne and powdered orchid,' he said solemnly. 'Good for love.'

He backed away, grinning. Lisa laughed aloud. Genuine laughter, no social pretence this time.

Kit turned indignant eyes on her. 'Did he mean what I think he meant?'

'Guess so,' said Lisa, bubbling over. 'Gosh, this place takes itself seriously. Get married here and you certainly get the full service.'

Kit looked at the hissing drink in dudgeon. 'Stop giggling. You mean you've just bought me an aphrodisiac?'

'Well, strictly speaking, Nikolai has just bought you an aphrodisiac,' said Lisa blithely. 'Tonight is going on his tab.'

'Great,' said Kit with irony. 'Just what I need.'

But Lisa was looking at the little card the waiter had brought with their drinks.

'Look, they've even got a map for a moonlit walk,' she said, awed. 'Everything the nervous honeymooner could want.'

'No honeymooner is nervous these days,' objected Kit.

Lisa looked wise. 'Don't you believe it. Every honeymooner is nervous.'

Kit looked unconvinced.

'Oh, come on, Kit. Think about it. The moment you get married, you've burned your boats. You're not nervous, you're *terrified*.'

'Were you?' asked Kit, curious at this unexpected revelation. She had never thought anything could terrify her sister. Lisa had been punching her weight since she was seven. 'Really?'

'Oh, yes. All the time. Every time Nikolai left me alone for a moment I went into a panic.'

Kit pursed her lips. 'Sounds like another good reason for not getting married.'

'You get over it,' said Lisa drily. 'And there are compensations.'

'I'll take your word for it.'

Lisa sighed. Kit braced herself to withstand a lecture on her empty love life. But Lisa was thinking about another subject entirely.

'I only had to look at him then...' The low tones were ineffably sad. It was almost as if she was talking to herself.

Kit could not bear it. She picked up the turquoise potion and took a long swig.

'Well, if I start assaulting the talent, I'll hold you responsible,' she said brightly.

Lisa shook off her shadows. She laughed.

'Not a lot of talent to choose from. The hotel is stuffed with grey men in suits. Middle-aged economists and paunchy academics to a man.'

Kit sat bolt upright. 'No, they're not,' she said indignantly.

'Well, apart from Nikolai—' Lisa broke off, rather suddenly.

Too late Kit remembered that she had unwarily told her sister about the man at the lagoon. Lisa might tell her never to get married in a moment of despair. But in reality she was concerned that Kit continued to avoid dating. She said so, frequently.

I should never have told her, thought Kit, irritated.

She took another drink. 'This tastes like shampoo.'

But again she misread her sister. Lisa was looking over the top of the hedge fixedly.

'Nikolai,' said Lisa in a strange voice. 'He's made it after all.'

A tall, dark figure was standing in the archway under the Chinese lanterns. He scanned the bar area in one quick, dismissive movement. Then he set off purposefully, pausing at the entrance of each bower for just as long as it took him to discover his wife was not there, before moving on.

Time I was not here, thought Kit, watching his methodical approach. She picked up her glass and stood up.

'I'm sure he's put the wrong stuff in this,' she announced. 'No one would *pay* to drink shampoo. I'm taking it back to the bar.'

'Fine,' said Lisa.

Kit had the impression that if she'd said she was going to slap a power pack onto her back and try to fly to the moon, Lisa would have said exactly the same thing.

She was watching Nikolai, too intently. She sat as still as a mouse, waiting for him to find her. And she made no attempt to help him.

Definitely time Kit was not there.

Lisa did not even notice her go.

Philip had not even realised that he was looking for the girl. For four days he had put her out of his mind. Well, nearly. But as soon as he saw her he knew that he had been waiting for her.

She came out of one of the box-hedge bowers with a glass in her hand. She walked as she swam; gracefully, powerfully. She was quite unselfconscious. She seemed to have no idea that anyone was looking at her, though Philip was not alone. Both the other men at his table paused, watching the tall blonde with her easy, athletic stride and her proud profile.

Philip was aware of a sudden stab of possessiveness. They had no *right* to watch her. They had not helped her out of the water. They had not told her about the ocean's fireflies. Or made her laugh. Or been invited to join her in the water.

Or kissed her.

He stood up abruptly.

'Excuse me. I see a friend over there.'

He left them before they could say anything.

'Signs of life, at last,' murmured the Frenchman, amused and rather impressed.

But Fernando looked after his boss with a worried expression. 'That is *so* not like him.'

'Oh, come on. What's the harm? There's no more he can do tonight. Why not kick back and enjoy? Tropical island, balmy breezes, pretty girl. You'd be inhuman to pass it up.'

'You don't understand,' said Fernando. 'Philip Hardesty *is* inhuman.'

But the Frenchman was watching the little tableau. The girl was moving fast, but Philip stopped her with only a word. She turned to him. Her face lit up as soon as she saw who it was.

Fernando turned his head. So he, too, saw Philip take the glass away from her with a smile. The smile went all the way to his eyes.

'Oh, no, he isn't,' said the Frenchman, a connoisseur. He gave a sigh that was nearly envious. 'Tonight he's as human as you get.'

'Hello again,' said Philip.

The girl turned to him almost eagerly. She

seemed to have forgotten that she had plunged back into the sea and raced away from him the last time.

'Hello.' It was that husky voice that had been haunting his dreams.

His pulse quickened in response. He did not let it show.

'Where are you taking that drink? Down to the shore?'

'Back to the barman. I can't drink it,' the girl confessed. 'It's supposed to have powdered orchid in it. But I think it tastes filthy.'

He smiled and took it away from her.

'Then let me get you something you can drink. Unless you're waiting for someone?'

Her eyes lit with laughter. She shook her head. The rainbow colours of the Chinese lanterns danced over it, turning it to gleaming gold. Her fairy-story hair fell over her shoulders and down her slim back like a princess's cloak. He thought of the unicorn again.

'Well, I was. Only he's arrived and I'm a gooseberry.'

He was astonished at the relief he felt. 'You're here with a girlfriend?'

'My sister.'

He led the way to the bar. He was tempted to put his arm round her. But it was too soon, too public. He was not sure how she would respond. She had run away last time, after all.

But she was glad to see him. And she was free for dinner, by the sound of it.

Play it carefully, Philip.

He attracted the barman's attention without even raising his hand.

'The lady doesn't like your concoction, Sariel. Give her—' He turned to the girl with one eyebrow raised. 'What would you like? Something familiar? Or another experiment?'

She hardly hesitated. 'Another experiment.' She gave a soft, excited laugh. 'This seems to be my week for new experiences.'

He cast an experienced eye down the drinks card and rejected all of them.

'Bring me rum, mango juice, angostura, that nutmeg you've got over there and some fresh limes,' he said. 'Soda water and a mixing jug.'

Grinning, the barman did as he was ordered.

'Mango is wonderful but it can cloy.'

Why did he always end up sounding as if he was a schoolmaster? Had he forgotten how to talk to women who attracted him? he thought, annoyed with himself. He gave her a deprecatory smile.

'That's what the guy who taught me how to make this said, anyway. The lime is supposed to cut through the sweetness and the rum gets rid of the vegetable taste,' Philip explained, working neatly. 'So all you're left with is that scented fruit. Then the soda water makes all these tastes explode on the palate.'

What am I doing? I want to take her into the shadows and find out if she feels what I feel. And I'm giving her a lecture on tastes!

He couldn't seem to stop. 'You know there's a legend that says the apple in the Garden of Eden was really a mango?'

The girl did not seem to have any criticism of his subject matter. 'Paradise fruit,' she said, as if she liked the idea.

He stirred the mixture briskly and pushed her glass across to her. 'Try it.'

She sipped. She looked like a girl who took her new experiences seriously.

'It's very—exotic,' she said carefully.

Philip laughed, throwing his head back with delight.

'You don't have to drink it if you don't like it. Have a nice, safe beer instead.'

She shook her head. 'I don't want a nice, safe anything. What's the point of coming to a tropical island and playing safe?'

Philip's pulse took another few seconds off its resting rate. But he kept it under control. He was good at that, after all.

'Feeling reckless, are you?' he teased. He sounded detached, amused. He was proud of that.

The girl twinkled shyly at him. Her eyes were a strange colour. Grey? Green? He'd have to get closer to be sure.

'Not reckless, exactly,' she demurred. 'Maybe—braver than usual.'

For a moment he thought a shadow touched her face. But then it was gone. He was not certain it had even been there. These lanterns cast a deceptive light.

He said lightly, 'Brave enough to have dinner with me?'

Not very original. Well done, Philip.

He found he was holding his breath for the answer.

She looked down at the nutmeg-dusted froth of her cocktail. 'Dinner? Where?'

'Anywhere you want. As long as it's somewhere in the hotel complex.' He was carefully unconcerned. 'The nearest pizza parlour is twenty islands away.'

She smiled at that. 'Pass on the pizza.'

'Then eat one of the local curries here with me.'

'Paradise curry?' she laughed.

'Exactly,' he said, smiling back straight into her eyes.

He saw the effect it had. Her eyes—those strange eyes; now they looked almost golden for a moment—widened. Then they fell and he saw that she had the longest eyelashes in the world. They lay on cheeks as soft as a child's. It startled him.

How young is she, for heaven's sake? What am I doing?

He said with sudden constraint, 'Of course, your sister and her friend must come too.'

'He's her husband. And I think they really need to be on their own.'

'Oh.'

Philip did not know whether to be glad or sorry.

Actually he was feeling as uncertain as a schoolboy. He could not remember when he had last felt like that, if ever. Even as a schoolboy he had always known what he wanted. This ambivalence was new. All his training taught him to deplore it. But in practice, it was rather exciting. Like suddenly being a student again with all his life before him. All his options still open.

It was like being free.

So when she said, 'I'd really like to have dinner with you. Thank you,' he silenced his uneasy conscience.

'Wonderful. Beach barbecue or the terrace restaurant?'

She pulled a face. It was clear that she had been to both and not liked either.

'The terrace is a bit much. All those waiters.'

He agreed. 'I ate there the night we arrived. There were more waiters than people eating. *Marie Celeste* time. All those empty tables set for people who weren't going to come. Unsettling.'

She shuddered reminiscently. 'And the way the waiters whisper all the time. As if they're in a library or something. Makes me feel as if I shouldn't be there. As if they know I'm not really grand enough.'

His eyebrows rose.

She pulled a face. 'Anyway, I thought it was creepy!'

'Right. Barbecue it is.'

But she still looked dissatisfied. Philip cocked an enquiring eyebrow.

'No?'

'We-ell, that's a bit grim too. Lots of middle-aged men eating in double-quick time so they can get back to their computers. It's not—you know—relaxed.'

Philip winced. That was exactly what he would have done tonight if he had not caught sight of her. 'Yes, I can see that.'

He thought. A picture presented itself—of the two of them calling Room Service and eating on his terrace above the ocean. They would look at the moon. And then they would—

He rejected it. He had never taken an unknown woman back to his room. He was not going to start now. It would be unfair to both of them. And a betrayal of those eyelashes, he thought wryly.

So he said briskly, 'All right. What about this? We get Room Service to pack us a picnic and we take it on the beach.'

She nodded excitedly. 'Or the cascade.'

Philip was blank. 'What?'

She picked up one of the little folded pieces of paper and flicked it open. 'Moonlight walks,' she said, tapping her finger on the little sketch map under his eyes. 'There's this wonderful waterfall round the cliff. They've got a place you can sit and watch it. I've been there every day. But at night it would be amazing.'

Philip felt a dark trap open in front of him. Oh, those *eyelashes*!

She did not seem to have any natural wariness at all. She seemed serenely confident that he was to be trusted. But was he?

'Do you think that's such a good idea?'

She looked blank for a moment. Then she nodded. 'Oh, you mean it might be closed because the hotel is so empty. Lisa was saying that they've cancelled a lot of their services. But surely a path is a path?'

'They may not have kept it in good repair,' said Philip, seizing the excuse gratefully. 'It might not be safe.'

He knew damn well it wasn't safe, not for either of them. Why didn't she?

Or did she, and didn't care? Had she had second thoughts about her flight from him the other night, perhaps? Did she recognise the chemistry between them, after all? And was this her way of telling him that she wanted to explore further?

Or was she completely unaware of the sizzling attraction?

To Philip it was electric. His head buzzed with it. But she gave no sign of feeling the same. It could be that she was just exactly what she seemed on the surface. Friendly and naïve and too gorgeous for her own good!

She said, 'Well, then, ask.'

Ask? For a moment his thoughts whirled wildly. *Ask what? Something like: do you know the risk we're running here, you and I? We're strangers. You don't know it but this is no time for me to get personally involved with anyone. You haven't even asked my name. Why haven't you asked my name?*

And then she leaned confidentially towards the barman and he realised that he had misunderstood totally.

'Is the path to the cascade safe at night?'

The barman looked from her to Philip's shuttered face and back again. He grinned.

'Very beautiful. Very sweet.'

Thank you, thought Philip ironically.

He wanted to go. He wanted to go so much. He could not remember when he had last wanted anything so strongly.

But, quite apart from the distraction she presented, there were the bodyguard's warnings. If he took her on this moonlit picnic, would he be putting her in danger? For himself he would be glad enough to meet Rafek again. It would be a chance to persuade him back into the talks. But this girl was another matter altogether.

He found he wanted to keep his unicorn-girl safe quite desperately.

Playing for time as he weighed the risks, he said, 'It's properly lit? No dark corners where we could fall into the sea?' *Or where enterprising guerrillas could hide?* Though of course he did not say that. 'No hidden hazards on the pathway?'

The barman reassured them in some detail. The girl turned wide eyes on him.

There I go again. Sounding like a schoolmaster, thought Philip in acute self-disgust. *She'll think I'm a complete wimp.*

Something in him revolted at the idea. It might not be sound and sensible. It might be out of character. It might be criminally irresponsible, even. But she had said it herself, hadn't she?

I don't want a nice, safe anything. What's the point of coming to a tropical island and playing safe?

For once, he wanted to forget he was a calm, judicious negotiator. Just for tonight he wanted to behave like a *man*.

Philip bowed to the inevitable. 'All right. All right. I'll buy it. The path is lit like Times Square and as smooth as an airport runway,' he said ruefully. 'Can you arrange some food for us to take? My companion fancies some exercise.'

But Sariel could do better than that. He would get the food delivered to the grotto.

'Grotto?' echoed Philip, all his misgivings leaping back.

The girl laughed.

'It's just a few rocky bits for people to sit on while they picnic,' she said. 'Not exactly a romantic hideaway.'

Philip looked down at her and found her face so full of genuine amusement that he thought, *Of course she knows what she's doing. Of course*

she does. I've just been out of the game too long.
I've stopped reading the signs properly.

He smiled back. 'Then let's go.'

The path was as beautifully lit as the barman had promised. There was a neat line of light bulbs set along the edge of the path. Each one was encased in a protective hood. The path itself was covered by well-raked flakes of bark, except for a couple of places where the underlying stone broke through. Roots of a couple of massive banyans were traversed by boards. The moment the slope got too steep, steps had been constructed. The most distracted honeymooners would not have missed their footing on that path.

'Sariel was right. This has been very well done,' Philip acknowledged, climbing steadily.

The girl ran lightly up a few steps to an outcrop, looking out to sea.

'Haven't you been up here before?' she said, surprised.

He pulled a face. 'No time. I've been working continuously, I'm afraid.' He drew a long breath and told the truth. 'I'm one of those middle-aged men who bolt their food at the beach barbecue,' he admitted ruefully.

She looked down at him. The stars seemed to wheel about her head.

'You're not middle-aged,' she said in that husky voice.

'Oh, I am. Older than middle-aged. I sometimes think I'm older than Methuselah. Hatred ages a man,' Philip said harshly.

He stopped, shocked at himself. He had not realised he felt so bitter.

She did not seem shocked, though.

'Hatred?' she said slowly. 'Who do you hate?'

'Me?' He was curt, instantly regretting his slip. 'No one.'

'Who hates you, then?'

He shrugged, not wanting to answer. Not wanting even to think about the answer.

To stop thinking about it, he said, 'Just look at that moon.'

It was enormous, and seemed very close, as if it was closing in on the earth deliberately to examine its handiwork. It was fuzzy at the edge, like a gossamer puffball. The sea breeze drove fast little clouds across it.

'Witches are riding tonight,' he said softly.

She was disconcerted. 'What?'

'It's what my nanny used to say. When there's clear night and a strong wind. Low cloud can look like figures on broomsticks, I suppose.'

They resumed climbing. The girl did not answer for a moment. When she did, he was surprised.

'Did you have a nanny, then?'

'Several.'

He thought of the succession of nannies, the stern, angry ones; the young, anxious ones; the ones who taught painting and the ones who made him learn spelling for hours; the ones who forbade him to go beyond the nursery wing and the ones who played games of tag with their lonely charge round the empty, echoing rooms at Ashbarrow.

'Oh.'

He sensed withdrawal.

'Do you have moral objections to nannies, then?'

'No.' She sounded subdued.

'My parents were away a lot of the time,' he offered, as if he needed an excuse. 'My father was a diplomat. He was posted to some unhealthy places. My mother went with him but she wanted me safe at home.'

'A diplomat,' the girl said in a hollow voice. 'Weren't you terribly lonely?'

Philip was puzzled. 'The nannies were quite kind,' he said comfortingly.

She didn't say anything.

He said teasingly, 'That sounds as if you suffered from an ogre nanny.'

She gave a snort. 'Not in this lifetime.'

He was even more puzzled. 'Well, then—'

She stopped in the middle of the path and looked at him, hands on hips.

'No nannies. No diplomats in the family. No father, to be honest. My mother has worked hard all her life but, frankly, we lived in a slum until my sister turned out to be a financial genius. She's married a man with—oh, with ancestors and furniture and stuff. But basically Lisa and I—we're trash.' She stuck her chin in the air. 'I wouldn't want you to get the wrong idea.'

He was shaken. Not so much by what she said as the ferocity with which she said it.

He said quietly, urgently, 'No one is trash.'

She looked at him with hot eyes. 'Would you say that if a member of your family was marrying me?'

'If a member of my family was marrying you I'd probably poison him,' Philip said coolly. Deliberately.

She had not seen it coming. It stopped her dead in her tracks.

'Oh!'

She was enchanting in her astonishment. Oh, those *eyelashes.*

This time he could not help it. The temptation was too great. He put his arm round her. She did not resist.

'Come on,' he said gently. 'Let's get to this grotto of yours. Then you can tell me all about it.'

CHAPTER FOUR

'THE path is steeper than it seems by day,' said Kit. 'But it doesn't seem to be so far. I know that tree. We're nearly there. How odd.'

'When you come here during the day you must keep stopping to look at the views,' the man said quietly.

He had said he was as old as Methuselah but he was not even breathing hard after that steep climb. Kit was.

And by day you're not holding my hand.

She did not say that, of course. He already thought she was enough of a fool. She had seen his wariness when she'd mentioned the moonlight path. He had thought she was contriving some phony romantic interlude until she put him straight. He had nearly not come up to the waterfall with her. She knew that.

And then her riff about nannies back there! What was she thinking of? *Fool,* she castigated herself silently.

This is a grown-up man, Kit. Why should he be interested in you? Or your hang-ups? Get a hold on yourself.

He was not holding her hand because he had been swept away by the beauty of the moonlight. He was helping her up the steep path. And if she was breathing hard, that was all the more reason for him to think he had to keep on helping her.

Catch twenty-two, thought Kit with grim amusement.

Here was the first man to make her heart beat faster in years. And if he knew the effect he was having he would head back to base at light-speed, just like Johnny had. It was as plain as the nose on your face. So she had to keep these feelings under control. She *had* to.

Struggling for normality, she said in a practical voice, 'Do you realise I don't know your name?'

'Yes,' said the man unhelpfully.

Kit stopped dead. It gave her an excuse to re-move her hand from his. Which helped her breathing but not her well-being. She suddenly felt appallingly lonely. It was ridiculous, of course. But the loneliness hit her like a tidal wave.

To disguise it, she said disagreeably, 'Are you going to tell me or not?'

He seemed to hesitate. Then he said carefully, 'I'm Philip Hardesty.'

Kit recognised the care. She bridled. 'Is that supposed to mean something to me?'

'No.'

But she did not believe him. 'You're famous, right? What do you do? Climb mountains? Save apes?'

He was startled. 'No. Why do you ask?'

Kit began to climb again. 'Because that's what my brother-in-law does. He's here on some save-the-rainforest kick. He said everyone else in the hotel was at the conference too.'

'He's right in a way,' Philip said. 'At least, there is a series of what you might call inter-locking conferences. We talk to each other but we're not exactly doing the same thing.'

'So what are *you* doing?' She thought about that first night, when he had had his hands on her and she had wanted— She said hurriedly, 'You're a naturalist, right?'

'In a way,' he said unhelpfully. 'Now I've told you my name, what about yours?'

She was oddly reluctant. It felt like giving him a bit of herself. And she was not sure she wanted to give him anything more than she had already. Only he didn't know about that, of course. He did not know he was the first man she had let touch her for two years. He did not know that she wanted him to touch her again. And it scared the hell out of her.

She said curtly, 'Catherine Romaine.'

'Catherine? Is that what they call you?'

Even more reluctantly she said, 'My family call me Kit.'

'Nice to meet you, Kit.'

She nodded, not speaking.

They had come to a curve in the path that she particularly loved. It was the last one before the grassy platform from which you viewed the waterfall. You could hear the water but it was hidden by the angle of the cliff. Ahead, the path looked as if it broke off, and there was nothing between you and the sea and sky. Beside you, a wild mango tree leaned against the cliff. And up through the branches of the mango twined the leafless canes of some flower that poured down, blossom upon prodigal blossom, filling the air with heady perfume.

The flowers were a dark tangle in the moonlight, of course. But Philip Hardesty caught the sweet scent. His head came up and he looked sharply up the cliff.

'Wonderful, isn't it?' Kit said softly, forgetting her constraint in sheer wonder. 'Sometimes I just come up here and breathe it in. Makes me feel I'm purifying my lungs.'

He expelled a long breath. 'I thought someone was there,' he said. To her astonishment, he sounded as if the idea made him uneasy. He took a long sniff. 'It smells like a woman's scent. What is it?'

She showed him the flowers. He lifted one, touching his fingers to it so gently that it seemed as if the bloom was stirring in a breeze rather than being manhandled.

What would it be like if he touched her like that? The thought came from nowhere, shockingly explicit. Kit trembled and retreated a little. How embarrassing if he picked up her feelings.

No, more than embarrassing. Excruciating. And she was so bad at hiding them! *Lisa, why did you never teach me to put on that bright performance of yours?*

He turned the flower towards him.

'Purple, right? Or a deep lilac? That's the colour by daylight?'

She forgot her embarrassment in sheer surprise. 'Yes,' she agreed.

'Sangumay.' He sounded quietly pleased with himself for having made the identification.

Kit stared. 'What?'

'One of the most highly scented orchids. Not rare. But the scent makes it really exceptional.'

Kit made a little noise of exasperation. 'Why do you have to *label* everything all the time?'

'What?'

'When I was swimming you had to tell me that the phosphorescence came from shellfish. Then the name of those amazing ultramarine birds.

Now this. Why can't you just enjoy something because it's beautiful?'

'I do,' protested Philip.

'No, you don't,' she said shrewdly. 'You want to classify it and file it away. I bet you're really, really tidy.'

'I am, as a matter of fact,' said Philip, annoyed. 'It's not a hanging offence.'

'Then it should be,' said Kit with intensity. 'Look around you. You shouldn't be filing this. You should be living the moment for all it's worth. Moments like this come round once in a lifetime.'

She surveyed the scene eloquently.

The sky was a black setting for the lemon-drop moon and the sharp shards that were the near stars. Beyond them, the great spiral of the Milky Way looked like the crystallised breath of some giant animal. At the horizon, black met black. But the sea was like shot silk where peacock's-tail viridian and cobalt flickered among the blackness. And, of course, it was a great shifting mirror, so they saw two huge moons, two Milky Ways, two infinities…

'It makes me feel so small,' said Kit. She was almost whispering. 'And safe.'

'Safe?' Philip looked at her in astonishment. 'Feeling small makes you feel safe?'

'It's no bad thing to be invisible.'

'That's an interesting point of view—'

She held up a hand. 'Stop it.'

'Stop what?'

'Filing.'

There was a small silence.

Then Philip said, 'All right. No more filing tonight.' She could hear the smile in his voice.

It made her exultant. And terrified.

She said in a high, artificial voice, 'The place where you watch the waterfall is just round this next bend. Come on.'

When they rounded the headland, she had no cause to complain. Philip stopped as if he had been shot, gasping.

The waterfall poured down rocks on the other side of a deep valley. It was silver in the moonlight. The spray was flung up into the sky like shooting stars. The air was no longer languorously warm but electric. Kit could taste it on her tongue like champagne.

'Good God.'

Kit was pleased with his reaction. But she could not resist teasing.

'Want to tell me how many tons of water that shifts a minute?'

'No,' said Philip with conviction.

Kit beamed in the darkness. 'Come and sit on the viewing platform. If you open your mouth you can taste the water in the air.'

She led the way, sure-footed and fast now that her goal was in sight. Only to stop dead when she got there.

She had said to him that it was just a viewing place, with no romantic trappings. She had even believed it. But oh, boy, had she been wrong.

'Oh, my lord,' she said, horrified. Embarrassment swamped her.

This time there were no orchids to distract him. And she gave up on even trying to hide it. She stood there, twisting her hands together, agonised.

He would think— He would think that she— Philip came up beside her.

'I don't understand,' she said. It was a cry of pain. And it was more to herself than to him.

'Ah,' he said. 'The grotto.' He sounded infuriatingly bland.

Kit turned, spreading her hands. 'I never realised— I didn't see— I'm stupid. I'm so sorry.'

'Sorry?' Philip sounded amused, too. He was clearly enjoying himself.

But enjoyment was not an option for Kit. She writhed inwardly. And it showed.

She waved a repudiating hand at the little temple that had emerged from the jungle undergrowth beyond the clearing.

'That wasn't here—I mean, I never saw it before—I mean, it must have been here but I didn't notice it...' She broke off, wringing her hands.

It was a rotunda, with supporting columns and a domed roof. Someone had lit hundreds of small candles inside it. They flickered gently in the softly eddying night air. The light turned the pale stone to gold.

So now Kit saw that what she had taken for trees and creepers were fluted columns. It was half-hidden by the lush vegetation, true. But it was manmade. Made, furnished and now illuminated by man for a purpose which was all too clear.

Damn this honeymoon island and the over-sexed imagination that had put it together.

She gave up on words. 'Aaaagh!'

Philip was even more amused.

'Live for the moment,' he quoted back at her maliciously.

But Kit was too upset to see any humour in the situation.

'What an idiot I am.'

Philip saw that she was on the verge of tears. He was touched.

'Hey. No harm done.'

'But—'

'It's all right,' he said soothingly. 'I see how it happened. Whenever you've been up here by day you've sat on one of those stones and looked out at the waterfall. That means you've had your back to the little temple of earthly delights over there.'

Kind though he obviously meant to be, he still sounded wickedly amused about that. Kit flushed in the darkness.

'Really, stop worrying. I never thought you got me up here to seduce me,' he told her.

He even managed to sound as if he meant it, thought Philip, pleased with his performance. The trouble was, he was not finding it easy to forget the moment when he had thought that was exactly what she had in mind. And how he had reacted.

Now he saw how wrong he had been. She was as distressed as if he had caught her going through his suitcase. He set himself to reassure her.

'Come on. Since it's the first time either of us has seen it, we can find out what's inside together.'

What was inside was a banquet. A carved low table. Food in silver-covered dishes. A great cornucopia of exotic fruits. Gleaming goblets. Wine. Water, sweet as nectar. And a rattan couch scattered with golden cushions.

Kit gulped.

'Ah,' said Philip, mastering his astonishment with more skill. 'Our picnic.'

'Picnic!'

'You were the one who vetoed the beach barbecue,' he reminded her. Unholy amusement quivered in his voice.

'I didn't mean I wanted this—this—' Words failed her.

'Over-the-top extravaganza?' he suggested, straight-faced.

'Tawdry set-dressing,' said Kit coldly.

'Would you call it tawdry?'

'And phoney. Just to—to—'

'Set the mood?' he supplied again, helpfully.

'Will you stop finishing my sentences for me?' said Kit between her teeth. 'This is ludicrous.'

Philip strolled forward. 'Looks rather good to me.'

He picked up the lid of one of the silver dishes and sniffed appreciatively.

Kit resisted the temptation to throw things. 'It's not *funny.*'

'Yes, it is. Relax. You don't want to seduce me. I don't want to seduce you.' *May God forgive the lie.* 'No one can make us do anything we don't want to do.'

She looked at him with hot eyes. In the flickering candlelight he could not guess at their colour at all now. But he saw all the little flames reflected in them. And her misery.

How sensitive she was. Too sensitive.

He curbed his amusement. And his regret. He said gently, 'Look, let's just sit down and have our meal. Then we'll go back down the cliff again and I'll do a couple of hours' work. By the time you go to bed tonight, this will seem like nothing. Just a meal that was a bit more interesting than a barbecue. You'll see.'

She came into the temple reluctantly, like a wild animal that kept a wary eye on its escape route all the time. And she sat awkwardly on the couch, as if she was afraid he would sit next to her. She looked ready to bounce to her feet the moment he approached.

Philip said with an edge to his voice, 'Relax.'

'How can I?' said Kit angrily. She looked round the temple with distaste. 'Any minute now one of those whispering waiters is going to turn up, isn't he? I mean, how did they get all this up here? No one passed us on the path. They must have someone up here. Waiting for custom!' She sounded furious.

Philip's head came up, arrested.

'What?' said Kit, alert to his change in mood.

'You're right, of course. Why didn't I see that?'

'What? You really do think there's someone up here?'

She tried to find it amusing. It was difficult. She had never felt so exposed.

That's what letting yourself respond to erotic fantasies does for you, thought Kit grimly. If Lisa had not told her about rose petals and harem couches appearing for lovers as if by magic, she would not now feel as if someone was standing in the undergrowth, spying on them. Or so horridly self-conscious.

She raised her voice, trying to make a joke of it. 'Come out, come out, whoever you are.'

Philip did not smile, though. He shook his head, eyes narrowed.

He said, 'Quiet!'

It sounded as if he was used to giving orders. Suddenly he looked like someone she did not know.

Well, that was crazy. She didn't know him anyway, did she? But she had felt as if she recognised him somehow. She had not exactly been comfortable with him. It was too spiced with uncertainty and sexual tension for that. But *right* somehow, as if they were in some sort of elemental harmony. As if her body recognised his body, maybe.

But, looking at him now, she realised that was an illusion. In spite of the warm night, she began to feel cold.

'What is it?' said Kit slowly.

'Nobody passed us on the path. There's got to be another way of getting up here.'

He went back into the clearing.

Kit sensed a sudden urgency in him. Nothing to do with her. Nothing to do with the hotel's erotic-fantasy service. She ought to be relieved, she told herself. Of course she was relieved. Suddenly there was no need to be embarrassed any more.

And they were a thousand miles apart.

She heaved a long sigh—of relief, she told herself, *of relief*—and followed him.

'What's the matter?'

'I think I may have been very stupid,' said Philip, more than half to himself.

The ankle-height lighting led to the temple and stopped at the steps, of course. He stepped off the illuminated path, into the undergrowth. He brought the small torch out from his pocket, and raked the heavy foliage cover.

It did not take them long to find it. It was a rough wooden cage attached to an even rougher pulley system. It came up the straight side of the cliff from the valley floor. Its landing place at the bottom must be only a few yards from the main hotel kitchens, Kit calculated.

She said so.

'Of course,' said Philip.

He prowled round the contraption, studying it. She watched him, brows knit.

'What is it?' said Kit again.

'It would be easy for someone to come up in the cage. With all the noise of the waterfall and the jungle wildlife, we probably wouldn't notice.'

'You mean, creep up on us when we aren't looking?' scoffed Kit, though her heart beat suffocatingly hard all of a sudden and she had to work hard to put all thoughts of rose petals out of her mind. 'Why would they do that?'

He gave her a quick, unsmiling look.

'I think I'd like to make sure it doesn't happen. Just in case.'

So he didn't want rose petals showered about them. Heavy-handed romance was out! Well, she was glad. Of course she was glad.

He began to winch the cage up from the valley floor. In spite of its evident age, the winch and pulley were almost silent. Philip raised his brows. He bent forward, examining the cogs.

'Thought so. This has been greased. And recently.'

In spite of her conflicting feelings, Kit's lips twitched. Romance was out with a vengeance, it seemed!

'Wow. When they set up a fantasy, they take it seriously.'

'Fantasy?' He was frowning. 'Oh, yes, of course. Fantasy.'

So he wasn't even thinking about rose petals! Kit shivered and put both arms round herself.

Philip stopped winding and peered over the edge of the cliff. The cage was about a quarter of the way up.

'That should do it.'

She strolled over, keeping a careful distance between them. 'Do what?'

'Distant early warning,' he said obscurely.

He produced a Swiss Army knife from his pocket and flicked open a stout blade. He went briskly round the plants, looking for dead wood. When he had a sizeable bundle he stuffed it into the winch.

'That won't hold it,' said Kit practically.

'It doesn't have to hold it. Just alert us when someone starts to winch it down.'

'Alert us?' She was startled and suddenly rather worried.

He seemed to realise that he was disturbing her. He shrugged and said lightly enough, 'I don't like surprises.'

But Kit did not believe in that light tone. It was the first time she had not believed something he said, she realised.

She must have looked sceptical because he frowned.

'Always cover your back,' he said crisply.

He snapped the Swiss Army knife together and stowed it in his pocket.

Kit swallowed. 'It's like being under siege.'

He did not answer that, just tested his device. As the balance changed, a few of the twigs broke with a crack like a pistol shot. Kit jumped.

'They won't creep up on us now,' said Philip with satisfaction. He saw her expression. 'Don't look so worried. It probably won't happen anyway. Forget it.'

'Oh, yes? Like you're going to forget it?' said Kit drily. 'We're going to be sitting here, waiting for the pistol to go off.'

He grinned. And suddenly he was the man she knew again. Or the man her body told her she wanted to know, anyway.

'No, we aren't. You're going to tell me the story of your life. I'm going to forget everything but that.'

He stood back with a flourish. The path to the temple was illuminated like a runway. Kit smiled and stepped onto it. Philip followed.

But she saw out of the corner of her eye that he took out a small mobile phone from his pocket and checked that it was switched on. Oh, yes, romance was definitely out. It had probably never been on the cards at all, except in her own self-deceiving imagination.

That's what comes of staying in a hideaway designed for lovers, Kit told herself ironically. That and too many tropical stars. It played havoc with the perspective.

She went back into the temple, struggling to get her perspective back into focus.

He had lost her, thought Philip. He was furious with himself, with the whole situation.

He had followed his instincts. All he had wanted was to be an ordinary man for a few hours. Who was he kidding? Hell, all he had wanted was to be a *man*. And all he had succeeded in doing was putting Kit Romaine in potential danger.

The best he could hope for now was that she would not realise it. And that he would get her back safe.

For a moment he had toyed with the idea of returning at once. But only for a moment. That path was too narrow. If Rafek's men were really intending to kidnap him, he could walk Kit straight back into their arms. And if they took the cage to the bottom of the valley, who knew what would be waiting for them when they got there?

No, much better to stay here, as if he had noticed nothing, and wait for his enemy to show himself. If there was an enemy, of course. Even now, he was not sure.

Whether there was or there was not, Kit must not be alarmed. His precautions had already made her jumpy. He could see that and he could not blame her. But he had to do something about it and fast.

If there turned out to be no danger, he wanted her to have an evening to remember. And if the danger was real—well, he needed her calm. So, either way, she must be charmed into relaxing.

Philip set himself to charm as he had never charmed before.

So when she said, 'That sabotage device looks very professional,' he gave her one of his best glinting smiles and shook his head.

'Not professional. Inventive.'

She sat down. 'What's the difference?'

'Professionals come prepared. Inventors have to use whatever is to hand.'

She relaxed a little, looking amused. 'Well, it's very clever.'

'Learned from an expert,' he said lightly.

That worried her again, he could see.

He added hastily, 'Before my father was seconded to the diplomatic service he was in the
army. He commanded a troop who specialised in
what they called dirty tricks. They used to show
me how it was done.'

'And you enjoyed it,' she said on a note of
discovery.

'Any small boy would enjoy it. But I like finding solutions to practical problems, yes.'

And the practical problem here was to get her
back to the hotel safe, without scaring her out of
her wits.

He surveyed the loaded table. The candles
flickered among the bright dishes, making it look
like some seducer's banquet. His mouth quirked
with wry self-mockery. Fat chance of that!

He picked up a tapered dark green bottle.
'Wine?'

She shook her head. 'Water for me. I'm
thirsty. And anyway, the wine is probably spiked
with powdered orchid.' It was a gallant attempt
at a joke.

Philip was impressed. He had seen how his
antics out there had scared her. Her determination to hide it touched him.

So he responded in kind as he poured her water into an over-decorated goblet. 'Why powdered orchid?'

'It's an aphrodisiac,' she said with a great air of expertise. Then flushed to her golden hairline as he raised his eyebrows. 'At least—that's what Lisa told me.'

'Well, we certainly don't need an aphrodisiac,' said Philip drily. He inspected the label on the bottle, then put it on one side. 'I think I'll pass, too.'

There was some guava juice. He poured sparkling mineral water onto it for himself. Then he flung some cushions onto the marble floor and sank down onto them. He clutched one arm round an upraised knee and surveyed her over the top of it.

'So tell me about yourself. What are you doing in this part of the world?'

Kit considered that seriously. 'I suppose I'm having a holiday.'

'You suppose?' He was intrigued.

'Well, it wasn't planned or anything. But my sister is here with her husband and he has turned out to be working all the time. So she called me to come and join her.'

He nodded. 'I see. So you're here as a lady's companion.'

She laughed aloud at that. 'You wouldn't say that if you knew my sister Lisa. She's not a lady's companion sort of woman at all.'

'But she still wanted company?'

Kit's laughter died. 'She's not been well.'

She was looking anxious again. He wanted to take her in his arms and smooth the worry lines from her brow.

'Hey,' he said gently. 'Not a lady's companion. More like Florence Nightingale. Or maybe St Joan.'

She looked startled. 'Good heavens, no. I couldn't go into battle to save my life. I'm just here to share the sunbathing.' She gave an affectionate smile. 'Lisa is the one who goes to war. She can't bear injustice.'

And she began to talk about her sister. Then her struggling single mother, with her limited budget and high ideals. Then, slowly, hesitantly, she began to mention herself.

This was important, thought Philip. He sat very still.

Kit was not used to talking to someone who listened so attentively—or without interrupting. Almost imperceptibly, she began to edge towards the difficult stuff. He did not interrupt. He did not exclaim. He did not seem shocked or, worse, sorry for her.

'You see, Lisa wasn't just brilliant. She was always so brave, too. And I'm a complete rabbit. At everything. Can't catch a ball to save my life. Can't sit an exam without falling apart. Never really been good at anything. And I get so *scared.* Total chicken. Lisa's never scared of anything.

'When I got into college I could hardly believe it. But I worked hard, at least to begin with. For the first time I wasn't a pale copy of Lisa. Can you understand that? I was never going to be brilliant but I didn't mind. I was *me.*

'I began to think I might be a children's librarian. I like books and I seemed to be able to interest children in the project work. I ought to have got that qualification. But then—'

She stopped. If he had prompted her in any way she would not have started again. She knew it. It had happened a thousand times, with friends, with kindly, bewildered therapists, with Tatiana, who was impatient, with her mother, who was frankly scared, with Lisa, who was sure she could put everything right.

But he did not prompt her. He did not ask anything. He just sat there, sipping his drink, and watched her with calm eyes.

Kit swallowed.

'There was a guy in my class. Sort of leader of the pack. He took me out a few times and then— Well, he had a real girlfriend. She was at another university. Only I hadn't realised that. By the time I did, I was hooked.'

Still he did not say anything. He went on not saying anything for longer than she would have believed possible.

Kit burst out, 'It was horrible. I was like a puppy, following him around. It was as if I couldn't stop myself. He was quite kind to begin with, I suppose, and then—' She stopped, swallowing. No, she was not quite ready to tell *that* yet. 'I suppose he'd just had enough. He told me to stop fawning on him. He said it was gross. I felt—disgusting.'

She had never told anyone that before.

He stayed calm, though, neither exclaiming nor sympathising. Instead he nodded, as if both she and Johnny had behaved in a perfectly reasonable way.

'It's all right to be in love with someone who isn't in love with you, you know,' he said levelly. 'It takes time to work that out, of course.'

Kit stared.

His smile was rueful. 'We've all done it. It's not terminal and it's not shameful. You just have to accept it. Then let it go.'

She said gropingly, 'Are you saying that you've been in love with someone who didn't want you?'

He shrugged. 'Who hasn't?'

She shook her head. 'Just about everyone I know.'

'Then you can't know them all that well,' he said drily.

'But—'

It seemed he felt she had talked about it enough. He stood up.

'Hungry? That curry seems to be calling me.'

Kit looked up at him. 'You've just said the great tragedy of my life is ordinary.' She did not know whether to be affronted or to laugh.

He took a plate and put some rice on it.

'Do you like spicy food?'

Kit was hardly paying attention. 'Sure.' She hated it. 'Did you hear what I said?'

He smiled at her. It was a smile you might give to someone you loved, she thought, blinking.

'I said the great tragedy of your life was ordinary,' he repeated obediently. 'Sorry.'

Kit found that she wanted to laugh after all. It was wonderful.

'I should think so too,' she said severely. 'When did you work that out?'

'That falling in love with people who don't love you is normal?' He thought about it. 'I think I always knew it.' He gave a sudden grin. 'Maybe all guys do. My father's advice on sex consisted of him staring out of the window and telling me I'd get turned down a lot.'

Kit gave a startled hiccup of laughter.

'And did you?' she said curiously. She could not imagine it.

He put his own food on a plate and sat down among his cushions again.

'Enough,' he said wryly and began to eat.

Kit nibbled a forkful of rice and curry. She noticed the aromatic warmth on her palate almost absently. She, who never ate anything without pacing herself through every mouthful!

'And it didn't hurt?'

'Yes, of course it did. Hurt like that is part of growing up.'

She digested this in silence.

'You're very grown-up, aren't you?' she said sadly.

Philip looked up. 'It happens to all of us.' He hesitated, his mouth wry. 'How old are you, as a matter of fact?'

'Twenty-two.' She sounded ever so slightly defensive. 'Does it show?'

He raised his eyebrows. 'You're an adult,' he said levelly. 'If you'd asked me to put an age on you I'd have said anything from seventeen to thirty. But then, I'm not good at ages.'

Kit only heard one word of that. *'Seventeen!'*

So he had thought she was an adolescent! And she had thought he was attracted to her! What a fool she was. What a fool he must have thought she was.

And then he said softly, almost to himself, 'Water nymphs are always seventeen.'

Arrested, Kit stared at him, forgetting everything but the look in those intense dark eyes. She saw his half-smile and could not interpret it.

She said uncertainly, 'I don't understand.'

He met her eyes. He was no longer talking to himself when he said, 'And wonderful.'

'What?'

'You probably don't remember. I came out to you when you were swimming.'

Kit scanned his face, disbelieving. His smile was crooked.

'You were so—*happy*. As if you lived in a different world. I wanted to get into your world so much.' He smiled. 'Who am I kidding? I wanted *you*.'

A strange feeling crept over her, part thrill, part sober. Was he saying he had wanted her? That when she had hugged that to herself she had not been wrong, after all? Kit sat up very straight.

'It's all right,' he said, misinterpreting. 'I'm not mad. I'd been sitting in a terrible meeting. We went round and round in circles and I knew I couldn't cut it short. And all the time I was watching you playing out in the lagoon. You looked a complete natural in the water. Like a seal or something, with all that phosphorescence flying around. As soon as the meeting broke up, I came out to you. I told myself I wanted to see if you were real.'

Kit sat very still.

'Is that why you kissed me?' she said before she could stop herself.

'I suppose so.' He shifted impatiently. For the first time he looked uncomfortable among his cushions.

She put her plate down.

'Philip—' It was the first time she had called him by his name.

'Yes?'

'Kiss me again,' said Kit, who did not let men touch her.

His eyes grew intent. Not breaking eye contact, he scrambled to his feet. He kicked the cushions away impatiently. Kit stood up to meet him.

For half a second—less—she thought, *I can't do this. I don't know how to get close to another human being without freaking out.*

And then found it was easy.

His arms were not imprisoning steel. They were hard, sure, but warm, living flesh. And they shook slightly. It was that tremor that turned her heart over.

Murmuring his name, she pulled his head down to her.

CHAPTER FIVE

IT WAS a long, questioning kiss.

His mouth was gentle. Slow and gentle and so confident that it made her head spin. He held her strongly but she felt supported, not imprisoned. He was a stranger but he felt as familiar as her own skin.

Even so, Kit waited for the crippling moment when suffocation would start, as it always did. It did not come. And still he held her, his mouth moving with voluptuous tenderness. With increasing disbelief, she began to realise that the suffocation was gone.

It felt as if an iron bar had dropped from her shoulders. She felt her whole body soften and mould itself to his. It was not like anything she had ever felt before. Her breath quickened.

Philip felt the change in her. It was as if she had come alive in his hands. His whole body surged in response.

Then his head took over.

He raised his head. 'This,' he said, 'is not sensible.'

134

In the crazy candlelight her eyes were enormous. They looked dazed.

'No,' she said uncertainly.

But she did not draw away from him. And, as he watched, her lips parted.

He wanted her so badly it was a physical pain. He clenched his jaw, fighting it.

'Not here,' he said roughly.

She did not seem to be listening. She put a tentative finger to the place where the muscle jumped in his taut jaw. It was a shy gesture, as if she had not done anything like that before and was not quite sure that he would let her. Yet it was oddly trusting. It nearly broke his resolve.

He stopped her, covering her hand with his. His grip was convulsive, stronger than he intended. He heard her little in-drawn breath of pain and was instantly remorseful.

'I'm sorry. I didn't mean to hurt you. But—'

'I know. Not here.' Astonishingly her voice was full of tender laughter, although he knew how shy she was. 'Well, I've got a hideaway cottage just made for lovers down on the beach...' She did not finish the sentence. She did not need to.

Philip's fingers tightened round hers until her hand throbbed. This time she did not make any sound at all.

Kit thought, *I don't believe I just said that.* She didn't care. She saw the look in his eyes. She was ready to take any risk to keep him looking at her just like that.

Philip said under his breath, 'It wouldn't be fair.' He wasn't talking to her. He sounded as if he was in turmoil.

But the look in his eyes didn't change.

Not taking her eyes from his, Kit took his hand and carried it to her breast. The elderly cotton was no barrier. He could feel the warmth of her flesh, the vulnerable peak of her nipple, as if she were naked. Kit saw his eyes flare as he felt it.

A glorious triumph shot through her. She flung her head back, the golden hair rippling in the candlelight. She saw his eyes watch the play of light over her hair and knew that he was unbearably tempted. She was fiercely glad.

'Live for today.' Although they were alone, it was no more than a whisper.

He smiled straight into her eyes. It was dazzling.

'Is that a challenge?' He was whispering too.

'You tell me,' she teased. 'I've never seduced a man by moonlight before.'

'You're doing just fine,' he said drily. But his breathing was uneven.

'Am I?' Where did she get the courage from to flirt like this?

'No one would guess you haven't done it before.'

She pulled away from him, pouting a little. 'So how come you're still on your feet?'

He touched her eyelid very gently. 'It's not easy,' he said with feeling. 'But—'

And then there was a crack like a falling tree. Kit gasped, her eyes suddenly alarmed. She shrank closer to him but she was not flirting any more.

'Your trap seems to have sprung,' she said, fighting for calm.

Philip heard the flutter in her voice, in spite of the brave face.

'It's all right,' he said reassuringly. 'It's either dessert or my friendly neighbourhood freedom fighter. Either way, I can handle it.'

'Your *what*?'

'Freedom fighter,' said Philip absently.

He disengaged himself and went noiselessly to the temple steps.

Kit padded after him. 'What do you mean?' she began hotly. Being angry with him was better than letting cold panic take over, which seemed to be the other option.

Philip held up a hand for silence. He led the way outside and looked cautiously down the cliff side. She followed.

The cage was still on its way down. Two men stood at the bottom, waiting for it. One of them was carrying a brass tray with an Arabic brass coffee pot and a couple of the little thimble cups, she saw. So they were hotel staff, Kit thought. She gave a sigh of relief.

Philip did not relax, though. He nodded as if that was what he was expecting. He said over his shoulder, 'Are you any good at climbing trees?'

She did not ask why. 'Yes.'

'Good.' He turned back to her. 'I want you to go and sit up a tree. Don't make a sound until I tell you.'

'But—'

'Just a precaution,' he said, maddeningly unexcited. 'Maybe completely unnecessary. Probably is. But humour me. For my peace of mind.'

Kit swallowed. 'But what's going to happen? I mean—what about *you*?'

Philip looked surprised. 'I can handle this. It's what I'm good at.'

Kit looked at him and saw that he meant it. He looked completely calm. No—more than that, he looked as if he was about to enjoy himself.

'Come on. That's a nice big banyan tree. Up you go.'

His hands on her waist were quite impersonal. Was this the man who had been melting her with his eyes only a few moments ago? Who had shaken under her touch?

Kit shook her head, bewildered. She felt the power in his arms as he held her up until she got a grip on a branch. She swung herself up three or four branches, then crouched against the great comforting trunk as the mechanical cage came closer and closer to the top of the cliff.

Kit took a firm hold of her branch and prepared to sit as still as she ever had in her life.

It seemed to take ages for the cage to clank its way up the side of the cliff. As its dark roof appeared Kit had a moment's panic, when she wished she could touch Philip. She folded her lips together and held her breath until she was brave again.

Of the two men who got out of the car, only one looked like hotel staff at this distance. The other wore chinos and a loose cotton shirt in a camouflage pattern. He looked tough and not very friendly.

And Philip stood still and waited for him.

'Good evening, Rafek,' he said calmly.

The other looked at him, black eyes narrowed menacingly. Kit felt sweat break out along her bare arms.

'Good evening, Englishman.'

They know each other, she thought. *They've met before and they know what's going on here. And I don't.*

'What do you want, Rafek?'

The other laughed. 'I said I would come to your talks.' He spread his arms wide. 'Here I am.'

'And always welcome,' said Philip courteously. 'But the talks start in the main conference room at eight o'clock tomorrow.'

Talks? What talks?

The intruder put his hands on his hips. 'Maybe I'd rather talk to you now.'

Philip stood his ground. 'Why should you want to do that?' he asked mildly. 'The timing is hardly ideal.'

Rafek looked round the clearing. 'Not alone, Englishman?' It was a jeer.

The waiter with his round brass tray looked worried. He muttered something to Rafek in the guttural local dialect.

'As soon as I realised that you were on your way up, I got rid of the woman,' said Philip coolly.

That was her, thought Kit, wincing. The *woman.* Negligible. Expendable. And she had poured out her heart to this man!

Rafek grinned. 'What have you done with her?'

Philip shrugged, not answering. 'Are you here alone, Rafek?'

'You think my men will come up that path and kidnap you?' Rafek taunted him.

Philip did not blench. 'Will they?' he asked in tones of mild interest.

The guerrilla let out a great belly laugh. 'I like you, Englishman. No. Not this time. I come to your talks. I want to tell you. Is all.'

'Oh? Then why are there three men behind me?' asked Philip neutrally. 'They are crouching under that liana just off the path.'

This time there was a distinct pause before the belly laugh. 'You got eyes in the back of your head?' said Rafek, plainly put out.

'No, but there's nothing wrong with my hearing.'

The waiter looked even more uneasy. Rafek quieted him with a word, then summoned his henchmen out of the shadows. They swaggered forward challengingly. They looked like real villains, thought Kit in her hiding place.

Philip showed no sign of recoil.

'Good evening,' he said, polite as ever. And to Rafek, 'You want these gentlemen to join the talks too?'

Rafek snorted in contempt. 'No one but me. They do what I say.'

Unseen, Kit shivered. She wished she was standing close to Philip. She wished it with all her heart. Not just because Philip made her feel safe. Because he looked so alone.

The thought shook her to the core. *He has always looked alone, since that first night when he kissed me by the lagoon.* It was a revelation.

Alone or not, he was handling the situation with masterly cool.

'Then perhaps you would tell them to go back to the valley floor and wait for us,' he was suggesting gently.

There was a dangerous pause. Kit held her breath.

He was clearly used to giving orders, she thought, bewildered. He sounded so calm, so courteous. Yet when he asked for something he expected it to be done. You could see it in the way the man Rafek reacted. He bridled but, in the end, he complied.

He jerked his head at the men, sending them in the direction of the path.

'Not that way,' said Philip firmly. 'I would prefer you all to go back the way you came.'

Rafek's chin came up. 'You don't trust me.'

They faced each other, the one fierce and probably armed, the other so tall and controlled. Yet Kit was not surprised when it was Rafek who backed down.

'Very well.' With bad grace, he jerked his head at the cage.

As soon as the men had climbed into it the waiter began to winch them down. Not taking his eyes off Rafek, Philip turned his head a little.

'You can come down. We're going now,' he said.

With a little shock Kit realised that he was talking to her. He sounded so indifferent. Surely he should show some concern for her? Surely he should at least call her by her name?

She slid down the tree, grazing her palms and not caring about it. She moved into the light. Just for a moment it blinded her. She stood there, blinking, wanting to run into his arms.

And Philip turned his back on her.

Kit could not believe it.

Now her eyes had adjusted, she saw that he had brought out the little mobile phone. He flicked it open and pressed buttons. Someone answered.

'Hardesty here.'

In spite of the name she would now never forget, he did not sound like her Philip. He sounded crisp and efficient and about as remote as the stars out there in the brilliant sky beyond his shoulder.

'No,' he said into the phone. 'No problem. General Rafek and I have got together after all.

Could you meet us? There's an elevator that goes up to the viewing platform for the big waterfall. You'll find three of his men already there. We'll be coming down in a few minutes.'

They could not hear what the man at the other end of the phone said but Philip smiled.

'No, that's not a problem either.'

He's talking about me, thought Kit. She felt chilled to the bone. So that was the extent of her importance, was it? *Not a problem!* And only ten minutes ago she had all but invited him back to her cottage. The sheer exposure of it made her shake convulsively. She felt naked. Worse than naked.

He glanced up and met her eyes. The light in the clearing was uneven but Kit had no doubt about his expression: total blankness. You would have thought he'd never seen her before.

This was more terrible than anything that Johnny had done to her, Kit thought numbly. This felt like total betrayal. How could she have been such a stupid, *stupid* idiot?

'*I've never really been good at anything…*' '*…a pale copy of Lisa…*' '*I followed him round like a puppy…*' Was there anything she hadn't told him? She had stripped herself so he should know her properly and now—

And now he was looking at her with complete indifference. It burned like ice, that indifference.

And I thought he was lonely!

She could have laughed aloud if she had not been afraid it would turn into tears.

Give me Lisa's playacting powers, she prayed. *Just until I can get away from him.*

He finished his call and snapped the telephone shut. 'Let's go.'

All the way down in the rickety cage Philip talked in a quiet voice to Rafek. Kit stood huddled next to the waiter, as far away from Philip as she could get. She did not look at him once. She kept her eyes wide, so they should not fill up with tears, and concentrated on the brass tray with its untouched coffee pot. As soon as they came to rest, she slid out of the cage.

Philip did look at her then. He broke off his conversation with Rafek to do so. Rather impatiently, she thought.

'I'll find someone to take you to find your sister.'

'No,' said Kit sharply. The chill was growing. 'No, I'm fine, thank you, Mr Hardesty.'

He stiffened and his eyes narrowed. 'But—'

'It's enough that one of us has been scared out of her wits,' said Kit, converting her hurt to anger and lashing out. 'I don't want to alarm Lisa as well.'

He was not listening to her. 'I'm afraid I must insist.' He was looking round for his assistant. 'Fernando will find someone to go with you.'

Kit gave him a glittering smile. 'I've got a few scratches that need attention. I'll go back to my cottage and break out the antiseptic cream. Why should I need anyone to go with me?'

'I would prefer it,' said Philip coolly. As if that ought to deal with all her objections.

Kit could have danced with fury.

Fernando was deep in conversation with the man she had seen with Philip before, the one in combat trousers with gold teeth. He responded to his chief's beckoning finger with a nod and began detaching himself.

Philip took her by the elbow and walked her away from Rafek.

'Please go with Fernando.'

Kit said blazingly, 'You're not a naturalist, are you?'

Philip folded his lips together. He hesitated. Then he said curtly, 'No.'

'Was anything you told me up there the truth?'

He looked momentarily stricken. Then that control shut down all expression. 'You'll have to be the judge of that yourself.'

Kit was shaking with rage. 'Great. I'll have to work really hard on that one,' she said sarcastically.

She thought for a moment that she had hit home. It almost seemed as if he winced. But then he turned to the approaching Fernando and she could not be sure.

'Philip?' said the assistant.

'Will you take Miss Romaine back to her room, Fernando? She rather got caught up in our games, through no fault of her own. See her safe home for me?'

As if she were a *parcel*, thought Kit, fuming. She planted herself squarely in front of him.

'Are you telling me I'm a target?' she threw at him.

Philip flicked a glance at Rafek's men. Then he looked back at her. Just for a moment his face twisted.

'No,' he said quietly. 'No, you're quite safe as long as you keep away from me.'

The chill went right through to her heart, as if she had been stabbed with a stiletto of ice. She wrapped her arms round herself protectively.

'Well, that's not a problem, then, is it?' said Kit with a wide false smile. 'I don't need an escort, thank you. I'll see you around. Goodnight.'

She did not break into a run until she was out sight.

Damn. Philip was furious with himself. He had hurt her. But until he was certain that Rafek did not have other men posted around the island, what could he do? If they thought she meant anything to him these guerrillas were quite capable of kidnapping her and trying to use her to sway his decision in the peace process. Pretending indifference was the only way he could think of to keep her safe.

But he could not expect her to see that. She did not even know what his job was, after all. She could not begin to appreciate how dirty some of the warring parties would get in their attempt to get the upper hand.

She just thought that he was rejecting her. Worse, she thought he had led her on to confide in him with cynical indifference.

And there was not one damned thing he could do to put it right. Not until the peace was signed, sealed and delivered, anyway.

He hated hurting her. He hated feeling helpless even more. He knew how sensitive she was now. She had tried to hide it but he saw how deep the hurt had gone. Just for a couple of hours he had had a chance with her. And now it was gone. She would not trust him again.

He would try. Of course he would. He would see her. Explain. But later. And later might be too late.

Face it, Philip! This evening could be the end of everything.

Damn, damn and double damn.

'Come with General Rafek,' he said between his teeth. 'You and I have a lot to talk about. And, by God, it had better be worth it.'

Kit got under the shower. It made her cuts tingle unpleasantly but that couldn't be helped. She needed to wash away the feelings.

What a fool she had made of herself! What a fool!

All those childish confidences. *I felt disgusting. I get so scared.* She had told him every last thing that she hated about herself.

And as for, *I wanted to be a children's librarian*! That just added a final touch of farce. She couldn't even manage a decent ambition like being a supermodel or an astronaut. What a prat he had to think she was.

Well, he had almost said it, hadn't he? Very kindly, of course. But even so, he had not pretended. *The great tragedy of your life is ordinary.*

'AAAARRRGH!' shouted Kit under the shower.

Well, let's just hope that I don't come face to face with him again, she thought. She did not think she could take the shame.

In the end it was an all-night session. Philip's minder stopped being the laid-back bodyguard and went onto full military alert. He talked into his short-wave radio and soon the hotel grounds were alive with silent men in combat gear.

Rafek was impressed enough to stop swaggering and set out his demands with comparative clarity. Philip took him through the agreement reached so far. Then released him to a suite that the hotel had rapidly made up.

Then Philip went back to the conference room. He knew there was no point in going to bed. He would not sleep. And he was all too likely to find himself sidetracked into planning how he could make it up to Kit.

When the delegates filed back in the next morning they found him heavy-eyed but in control. He had shaved and changed and his tie was straight but he still, if you knew him, had that indefinable jaded air that betrayed that he had been up all night. And he kept putting up his hand to his left eye.

The delegates were not interested in Philip's physical demeanour, though. What interested them was his companion.

'Gentlemen, I think you know General Rafek,' Philip said coolly. 'I am glad to say he has decided to join us. I think this marks a new stage in our discussions. Let us take it as a good omen.'

The talks moved onto a new plane. They got louder. Noisier. Violence threatened and Philip calmed it. Stubborn silence fell and Philip reminded them quietly of how much they had already achieved.

There were no breaks. Food was brought in. Messages were sent out continuously—for briefing, for instructions, for supplies. The delegates remained behind their closed doors.

Journalists began to drift back into the hotel over the afternoon. The grapevine had started to hum. Agreement was a possibility...was close...was a technicality away. Even the relaxed hotel staff seemed to catch some of the excitement.

In their cottage Lisa and Nikolai were being guardedly polite to each other as Nikolai's group awaited the results of the peace negotiations. Kit should have been glad. But she hardly noticed. She was too preoccupied with her own concerns.

The great tragedy of your life is ordinary.

Now that she had the time to think about it, that was quite encouraging. If it was not a tragedy then there had to be a chance that she would get over what Johnny had done, hadn't there? And if she could get over Johnny, who had taken six months of her life, she could get over a man who had taken less than six hours. Couldn't she?

Lisa, demanding an explanation of her cuts and abrasions, wormed the secret out of her.

'This is the man you met the first night?' she said gropingly. 'The sexy one?'

They were sitting under a palm tree on Kit's stretch of beach. It was late afternoon and they had lazed and swum and lazed again all day. Lisa had not said a word about Nikolai not wanting her any more. In fact, Lisa had been going off into little reveries with an expression on her face which made Kit suspect that her sister and brother-in-law were now comprehensively reconciled.

It was not something she wanted to ask about. Especially not with Lisa interrogating her about sexy men.

'Yes,' said Kit, going pink and furious about it.

Lisa pulled a face. 'Well, he seems to have handled it very well.'

'Oh, yes, he handled me brilliantly,' said Kit with bitterness. 'Let me talk like a twerp and then patronised me.'

'That's because he didn't lay a hand on you,' said Lisa sapiently.

Kit was indignant. 'Of course it wasn't.'

Lisa's eyebrows rose. 'So he *did* lay a hand on you?'

'Not in the way that you mean, no.'

'In what way, then?'

'Stop interrogating me,' yelled Kit, driven beyond endurance.

Lisa gave a small, cat-like smile. 'Welcome to the world, sister. It's about time.'

Kit would have retorted in kind but Nikolai came jogging along the beach to them. His hair was all over the place and he looked gleeful.

'Hardesty's put out a notice. Press conference in twenty minutes. They must have signed,' he said.

He flung himself down on the sand beside Lisa and gave her an intimate smile. 'You get me all to yourself from here on in, *mon amour*.'

Kit felt suddenly as if she was intruding. The physical affection between them was like a furnace. She found she was instinctively moving a little away from Lisa, away from their magic circle.

And then she heard what he'd said.

'Hardesty?'

Nikolai was taking Lisa's hand and carrying it to his lips. He said indifferently, 'The chief negotiator.'

'The chief—!'

Oh, no, thought Kit. So she had not only made a fool of herself. She had to go and make a fool of herself with the Head Honcho. She bit her lip so hard, she exclaimed with pain.

Lisa looked at her curiously.

Nikolai said, 'You won't have seen him. He's been locked up all week with the local brigands. But give the guy his due. He seems to have brokered a peace. And he's got us some agreement to monitor the primate populations. As long as we pay up, of course. But still, at least there's a chance of stopping the decline now.'

'Wonderful,' said Lisa, quite as if she had not been ready to wipe out personally every one of his beloved primates for most of the holiday.

He linked his fingers with hers. 'The conservation group have asked him to drinks tonight. He won't have time for anything else. But we want to say a formal thank-you.' He swung their linked hands gently. 'Will you come?'

Lisa smiled at him in a way which did not need words to convey acceptance.

'Great.' He stopped looking at his wife for long enough to say, 'Kit?'

'No,' she said in a hollow voice.

She couldn't face him. She *couldn't*. How could she have been such an idiot? She had even asked him if she should have heard of him. Why hadn't she dug deeper? Instead of prattling about herself like a self-absorbed teenager. Embarrassment crippled her!

She cleared her throat. 'No, I don't think so.'

'That would be a shame,' said Nikolai, who plainly didn't give two hoots as long as Lisa was looking at him like that.

But Lisa was a different matter. She swung round on Kit, frowning.

'Why on earth not?'

Kit wasn't prepared for that. She hadn't got an answer ready. So she fell back on the old one, the feeble one.

'I haven't got anything to wear.'

'Yes, you have,' said Lisa triumphantly. 'I know Tatiana made you bring her black and silver job because you told me so. You can borrow my cascade earrings and I'll put your hair up and hey presto. You'll be the prettiest girl at the ball, Cinderella.'

Kit wriggled. But it was hopeless. Lisa had made up her mind.

'Anyway,' she said in Kit's ear as she pinned long golden swathes on top of Kit's head later that evening, 'you'll almost certainly meet Mr First Night there.'

Kit gave a grim smile at the mirror. 'Why should I want to do that?'

'Because you noticed he was sexy,' said Lisa frankly. 'Gives him a head start over anyone else I've ever heard you talk about.'

Kit set her teeth and did not answer. Nikolai put his head round the door. He flapped a piece of typing paper.

'Here you are. Hot off the press. One of the journalists must have had a profile ready to go.'

Lisa took it. 'What's this?'

'Our guest of honour. Philip Hardesty, saviour of the rainforest,' said Nikolai and went off to the shower, whistling.

Lisa and Kit pored over it.

Sir Philip Hardesty is an aristocrat of the old school. An ancestor fought at Agincourt. Another was with Drake when he saw off the Spanish Armada. 'Half Europe has reason to hate my family,' this very twenty-first century gentleman says ruefully.

Kit let the paper fall. '*Sir,*' she said blankly.

No wonder he had looked so blank when she called him Mr Hardesty. She had thought—hoped—that he had noticed her rejection and was hurt by it. But it was simpler than that. She had just called him by the wrong name.

Lisa did not notice that she had lost Kit's attention. She was reading selected comments aloud.

' "New breed—talented operator—" '

'I'll say,' muttered Kit.

Lisa did not notice. ' "First rose to prominence in Tetlakhan when his boss had a heart attack," ' she read. ' "Possible academic career—universities are lining up to offer him a Chair in Conflict Resolution Studies—private life—" '

Kit leaned over Lisa's shoulder again, suddenly breathless.

Meanwhile, there's his private life. Ashbarrow, the Hardesty family pile in England, is a jewel of mediaeval architecture. And he hasn't been spending a lot of time there recently. New York-based friend, Soralaya Khan, says she wouldn't be surprised if he made some major changes in the coming months. Maybe it's back to Ashbarrow and the life of a country squire for this year's Mr Peace.

Kit gave a small moan. A stately home as well! No wonder he'd had all those nannies. It was the last straw.

'Don't be silly,' said Lisa, not understanding. 'It's not his fault he was born with a title. From the sound of it, he's a perfectly decent guy doing a first-class job. Just like Nikolai. I forbid you to get snobbish and prickly.'

Kit looked mulish.

'Anyway, he's the guest of honour. The ape-fanciers will be three deep. We won't get anywhere near him,' said Lisa blithely.

'I hope you're right,' said Kit with real feeling.

But, of course, she wasn't.

To begin with, Kit thought it was going to be all right. She slid into the room behind Lisa, doing her best to disappear behind pillars and tall men. Lisa accepted her excuse that she was uncomfortable in her borrowed dress. Up to this last week, it would even have been true.

But tonight she barely noticed how the stretchy stuff clung to her, outlining the curve of her breasts lovingly. Kit was way beyond self-consciousness about her body. Lisa's crystal earrings swung gently against her bare neck, reminding Kit constantly of the low neck of the dress. She was taller than Tatiana and the skirt revealed yards of bare leg, tanned to pale honey by the week's sun. And Kit was almost unaware of it.

She was breathing shakily and her eyes were restless. But not because she felt exposed by the dress. She felt exposed by her own unguarded behaviour. All she wanted to do was keep out of sight as long as she had to stay at the reception. And dive for the door as soon as she decently could.

She kept telling herself that Lisa was right. Philip Hardesty—*Sir* Philip Hardesty, curse his deceitful tongue—had bigger fish to fry tonight. He would not waste any of his time on a naïve idiot who had poured her heart out to him without stopping to think.

But Kit was not taking any risks. She located him as soon as he walked into the room. Lisa was quite right; he was surrounded by an eager group. It looked as if they were all talking at once. He stood with his head bent courteously, apparently untangling the conversation without difficulty. In total control, as always, she thought dourly.

Only then Kit saw him put out a hand to set down his empty glass. For a moment it looked as if he was going to miss the edge of the table. She saw him do a double take, and field the thing before it could fall to the floor. It was so quick that she could almost have convinced herself that she had not seen it. But then she saw him look round, carefully.

Checking to see whether anyone had noticed, she thought. Her brows knitted. What was going on?

But then that careful checking out of the room reached her quadrant. He frowned a little, turning his head as if he was trying to bring her into focus. And then, their eyes met. Locked.

Kit took off. She began to duck and weave like a professional to keep out of his line of sight.

Only to be torpedoed by her own brother-in-law.

'Here she is,' said Nikolai in self-congratulatory tones. 'Thought I'd lost you for a minute there, Kit. Thought you'd like to meet the great man. This is Philip Hardesty. My sister-in-law. Kit Romaine.'

Kit froze, perfectly horrified.

Then justified indignation kicked in. Would he have the effrontery to admit that he had already taken her on a trip round his particular merry-go-round?

He would.

'Kit and I have already met,' Philip said levelly.

He smiled at her. Nikolai's eyebrows hit his hairline. Kit met calm dark eyes and thought she would explode with fury.

'Well, not to say *met*,' she said sweetly. 'I didn't know you were the Big Cheese. You just forgot to mention it?'

Nikolai pursed his lips in a silent whistle. 'I'll just make sure Lisa's got a drink,' he said hastily and backed into the crowd.

Neither of them noticed him go.

'I'm sorry about that,' said Philip simply.

Kit strove hard to stay angry. It was a lot better than feeling a prize fool.

'Why didn't you tell me? Did you think I was too stupid to understand what you do?'

He looked startled. 'Of course not.'

'Then *why*?'

He shifted his shoulders. 'Because I didn't want to, I suppose. I do nothing but talk about deals and strategies and the terrible things people do to each other when they feel threatened. I wanted—'

'Time out,' said Kit, her voice catching.

'Yes, I suppose so.'

'So what does that make me? Mindless entertainment of the day?'

He was shocked into making a bad mistake. 'I didn't realise how sensitive you are until it was too late—'

Kit nearly took off, she was so angry.

She said between her teeth, *'I am not sensitive.'*

Philip promptly made bad worse. 'Then why are you tearing into me like this?' he said reasonably.

There was a moment when Kit, who loathed and detested scenes, genuinely thought she might slap his face. She saw his composed expression through a hot mist. All she wanted to do, she thought, was shake that composure to its foundations.

Then she took hold of herself. She'd made a fool of herself once. That was bad enough. Doing it again—and in front of her sister and brother-in-law—was a triumph she was not willing to accord him.

'I don't like cheats,' said Kit blackly. 'I never asked you to tell me anything. You didn't have to tell me lies.'

'I didn't.' His smile was a caress.

If he had but known it, that smile brought him nearer to a scalping than he had ever come in his adult life.

'I just left a few bits out. But I'll tell you anything you want to ask me.'

Kit drew a ragged breath. Her green eyes narrowed to slits of pure venom.

'All right,' she said dangerously. 'What were you intending when we went to the waterfall?'

He stiffened. 'What?'

'You said—at the time you said—that you weren't intending to seduce me. Is that true?'

Philip was an experienced negotiator. He recognised an elephant trap when he saw one.

'Kit—'

But she was too angry to let him finish. 'That newspaper was right when it said you were a talented operator,' she spat. 'Only I don't like being on the receiving end.'

'It wasn't like that,' said Philip, beginning to lose his cool for the first time in living memory.

Kit did not realise that she was the cause of a historical first.

'I know what it was like,' she said. 'I was there. Being a complete idiot for your amusement.'

He was very pale. 'You don't mean that.'

She swept on. 'Well, I hope you had a good laugh,' she said untruthfully. 'It's the last you get at my expense. Goodnight.'

She did not even notice the stares as she turned her back and left the honoured guest standing alone in the crowd. She did not see Lisa start after her with an anxious expression. She did not see Nikolai stop her.

She stamped back to her cottage in a black fury. The beauty of the night was lost on her. For the second night in succession she did not spare the stars a glance as she strode along the beach.

How dared he? Oh, how *dared* he talk to her in that patronising tone? Did he think he could pull her strings the way he pulled everyone else's?

Kit flung herself about the cottage, bumping into furniture and knocking over the waste-paper basket in her temper. Eventually her anger wore itself out. She found she was panting. She got herself some mineral water from the fridge and banged out onto her terrace.

The sky was black velvet. You could almost hear the stars singing. Along the beach, the palms rattled and whispered in the breeze.

Kit dashed a hand across her eyes. What good was a scented breeze to her? Lisa was right. The beauty of a place only made it worse when you were wretched. And she was wretched, all right. She could never remember feeling worse.

There were steps in the sand. She heard them, though they were almost soundless, just a soft pressure of substance on dust. Whoever it was was not hurrying.

Kit stood up. He would not dare. She went to edge of her veranda and looked.

Philip came, soft-footed, out of the darkness. She saw the gleam of his teeth. He was *smiling*. How dared he smile at her after making a fool of her?

He said quietly, 'Kit, we can't leave it like this.'

'You can do what you like,' she said rudely. 'I've already left it. Whatever *it* was.'

He said remorsefully, 'Oh, *love*. I never meant to hurt you.'

Kit blinked ferociously.

I will not cry, she told herself. I will not. I am not sad. I am ready to kill but I am not sorry for myself.

She said curtly, 'You haven't hurt me. And don't you ever use the word *love* to me again.'

There was a little shocked silence. Then he said in a constrained voice, 'I haven't done this for so long. I seem to be saying all the wrong things.'

'Try goodnight,' Kit advised him harshly.

He came up to the veranda steps. She stood at the top of them, barring his way. It was childish and she knew it. But she was shaking with anger. And something more than anger. That scented breeze, damn it. It smelled of falling rose petals. Or was that her overheated imagination again?

Philip gave a little nod. He turned away.

He's going! Kit thought in alarm.

Only then he dived sideways. Before she had realised what he was doing, he had vaulted over the wooden balustrade.

'Oh, impressive,' mocked Kit, though in truth she was breathless. 'I read that you like to keep fit.'

'Never mind what you read.' He prowled down the veranda to her, a tall, warm figure in the darkness. 'Listen to me.'

'Oh, have you got another story you want to peddle?' said Kit, deceptively affable.

But Philip had stopped trying to placate her. 'Don't be stupid. Everything I told you was true. OK, I left out a couple of things. What do you want? A full CV on the first date?'

'It was not a date,' Kit almost screeched.

'Of course it was,' said Philip.

And took her in his arms.

Oh, there were rose petals in the air all right. Rose petals and hot, hot spices and the sound of the sea. Or was it their thundering pulses? Come to think of it, which heartbeat was his and which was hers?

When he had kissed her by the lagoon she had slid through his hands like water, shy and unprepared. In the temple he had hardly touched her. Now she was not shy and she was not unprepared. And Tatiana's dress was no barrier.

His hands slid under the skirt, pushing it up her body as if the sophisticated jersey dress was some old T-shirt. His breathing was ragged, urgent. He flung her dress away, not lifting his mouth from hers. His hands on her spine were possessive, as if she was his and they both knew it.

Kit began to haul at his tie. She had never undone a man's tie before. She did not think she even knew anyone who wore one except Nikolai. She was horribly self-conscious. But she would not stop. She could not.

She was shaking so badly that if he had not held her clamped against his body she would have fallen.

She gave up with the tie, dragged it over his head and threw it as hard as she could. And then she began to reach for clothes she did understand—the cool of poplin and cotton, the little mechanisms of buttons and zips; she could deal with them. Especially when she had help.

And she had help.

He lowered her to the wooden floor of the veranda. He was murmuring her name over and over, his mouth against her skin, as if he could not believe that she was in his arms.

'Kit. My Kit.'

Her heart contracted. Her skin felt like silk where he kissed it.

Rose petals and spices and silk, she thought, her head spinning.

He shifted her against his body, made her aware of his desire, and then—slowly, slowly—deepened his kiss until it seemed they were fused together.

Kit was staggered at the depth of feeling that swept over her. Physical desire, yes. But more than that, an extraordinary sense of being at one with the universe, like the night and the wheeling stars over their heads. And so powerful, both of them.

She surrendered her last vestige of control and let him take her out among the stars.

It was only when she came down, shaken to the heart, she realised that she had travelled alone. She was not that innocent.

She raised her head, immediately anxious.

'What—what happened? Don't you want me?'

Oh, God, why did she always have to sound so pathetic?

'I mean—'

He touched a finger to her lips.

'I know what you mean. I want you all right.' His voice was strained. 'Maybe too much. But I wasn't prepared. I can't protect you.'

Kit let out a great sigh of relief. She had not realised she was holding her breath until then.

'I don't care.'

She began to curl around him, exciting him deliberately. He groaned, but he stilled her.

'I care.'

'But—'

'We have to be sensible. You'll thank me tomorrow,' he said. He sounded as if he was in pain.

It gave Kit confidence. She gave a soft laugh. 'But I believe in living for today. Remember?'

He shot away from her as if she had burned him.

'Enough,' said Philip harshly.

She stared, all the bright confidence snuffed out in an instant. He stood up and began to reach for his clothes with jerky, angry movements.

'I never meant to do this. I promised myself I wouldn't—' he muttered.

Kit's skin turned from silk to ice-cold leather at the words.

She scrambled to her feet. She was completely naked. It was the final humiliation.

'Will you please go?' she said in a wooden voice.

He looked up as if she had startled him. Didn't he expect me to have a voice? she thought, on the edge of hysteria.

Too late he realised what he had said. 'I didn't mean it like that.'

'Yes, you did,' said Kit, quite gently, still frozen. 'Goodbye.'

She went inside and closed the door. She leaned against it, shaking. She felt slightly sick. He had kissed her and held her and brought her to ecstasy. And he had never intended to make love to her.

This was worse than making a fool of herself. This was being made a fool of by a man she had, however briefly, trusted her body to.

This was the stuff of nightmares.

She called Lisa and Nikolai. 'I think I ought to go home tomorrow,' she said. She was amazed at how steady she sounded. 'Now that the conference is all done, you'll prefer to be here on your own for the last few days.'

Lisa's protests were half-hearted. Not that it mattered. Lisa could have torn her hair and beat her breast and Kit wouldn't have stayed a moment longer than the airline schedules imposed. She was never, ever risking coming face to face with Philip Hardesty again.

There was only one, last blow before she left. And she was not prepared for that for a moment.

She was waiting in the garden outside the hotel lobby for the helicopter to touch down. The azure bluebirds with their black frill tails were tearing into some fruit on the patio. Kit was glad that she was wearing her new sunglasses. Her eyes were so full of tears that she could barely see.

Lisa had gone to fetch her a paperback for the journey. Kit's roll-bag was on the grass at her feet. And one of the friendly hotel staff came down the steps to her.

'The Englishman? You have spoken to him?'

Kit shook her head.

'He looks for you.'

Kit swallowed hard and the brimming eyes cleared a bit. 'I doubt it.'

'He asked about a trip. For you?'

She shook her head, horrified at the way her heart clutched at the thought. 'No, that's impossible. I am leaving today. I am just waiting for transport.'

He frowned, dissatisfied. 'Excuse, please.' He went back up the steps a good deal faster than the hotel staff normally moved.

Kit concentrated hard on the birds. She could not remember what he had said they were called.

A voice said in her ear, 'Kit?'

She whipped round.

Philip Hardesty was wearing a pale grey suit and a perfectly laundered cream shirt. His tie was silk and his shoes almost certainly handmade. He looked the last word in international professional chic. And completely out of place in the tropical sun.

Kit retreated.

He said, 'I've left messages.'

'I know.'

'Won't you at least let me explain?'

'No explanations necessary,' Kit said crisply.

'Yes, there are.'

Unexpectedly he leaned forward and drew her sunglasses halfway down her nose.

'Green,' he said, as if he was answering a question.

She stared, not knowing whether to be indignant. 'What?'

'Your eyes. I was never sure.'

'My *eyes*?' Kit was outraged.

'And you've been crying.'

'Of course I haven't.'

He touched one gentle finger to the corner of her eye. The gentleness was nearly her undoing. He showed her the drop of moisture on the end of his finger.

Kit bit her lip. 'It's the sun. It makes my eyes water,' she said defiantly.

'Of course it does,' he said soothingly, patently disbelieving. 'I know you don't want to talk to me, Kit. But at least let me apologise.'

She stiffened. 'Apologise?'

Please don't let him talk about that night in the cottage when he didn't want to make love to me. I can cope with anything else. Anything but that.

He said ruefully, 'I've been in the peace-negotiation game a long time. I know the rules and I play the odds. There's a very small chance of someone like Rafek actually trying an abduction from the delegation itself.'

Kit pushed her sunglasses back up her nose, glad of their protection. 'I-is there?'

'Yes. And if I'd had my wits about me there would have been no question of it this time either.'

He touched her face as if it was precious. She flinched. His hand dropped.

'I put you in danger. Unforgivable.'

'You got me out of it,' Kit pointed out. Her voice sounded stifled. 'I forgive you.'

'Then you shouldn't. It was careless and un-professional.'

She stretched her lips in a cruel caricature of a smile. It almost hurt.

'Don't worry about it.'

'But I do. I was not fair to you.'

'Look,' said Kit harshly, 'I'm not on your con-science, right? We had a nasty moment and it's over. Forget it.'

Philip was not deceived. 'Look,' he said ur-gently, 'they do a day-trip on the hotel yacht. Come with me. Let's have a whole day together. Maybe I can make you understand—'

Kit had been reading the pamphlets in her cot-tage.

'The honeymoon cruise?'

Philip was taken aback. 'I suppose so.'

'I don't think so.'

'Please.'

He gave her that sweet, warm smile that made you feel you could see right inside him. And that he thought you were wonderful. Fraud, thought Kit, grinding her teeth.

'To make up for our interrupted picnic,' he said softly.

'Everyone would think we were lovers. If not honeymooners.'

He shrugged. 'So?'

That deadly indifference again, thought Kit.

'You don't care, do you?' she said, marvelling.

'Why should I?'

'Because it's not *true*,' she shouted, suddenly overcome. 'This crazy place! It's a fantasy world and every damned person here buys into it. Rose petals and lovers' hideaways and lining paper with wedding bells in the drawers.'

'What?' said Philip, pardonably confused.

She squared up to him, like Lisa in one of her most virulent terrier moods.

'Do you know what they would call us, the boatmen and the waiters and the chambermaids? The Englishman and his bride, that's what. His *bride*.'

His smile was lopsided.

'What's wrong with that?'

Kit didn't answer. She couldn't.

He took a step forward. His voice dropped. It was like a caress. 'Would it be so bad to be the Englishman's bride?' tempted Philip Hardesty alluringly.

Kit felt as if she had been punched in the stomach. She could not speak. She felt her face whitening. The garden began to spin. She put an uncertain hand out to steady herself. There was nothing to hang on to. She staggered.

Philip caught her.

She rounded on him.

'Let go of me! You don't have any respect for me at all, do you?' It was a croak.

Philip was startled. 'That's just stupid.'

'Don't call me stupid,' flashed Kit.

'I didn't,' he said, thoroughly confused. 'I mean, I did but not like that. Kit, you've got to listen to me—'

'Leave me alone,' said Kit between her teeth, 'or I will make the scene of the century.'

He did not, of course. He took her by the shoulders. And Kit broke out into peal upon peal of horrible laughter.

Lisa came running down the path. One look at Kit's face and she put a sustaining arm round her.

'It's all right. I'll look after her,' she said to Philip with finality.

He let Kit go reluctantly.

And then, most fortunately, the helicopter arrived.

Kit bundled up her roll-bag with clumsy hands and fled for it, Lisa pounding after her.

She leaned into the helicopter as the pilot stowed Kit's luggage and strapped her in. Her pretty face was worried.

'Kit, what is it?'

'I'm getting out of here,' said Kit. She sounded lethal. 'And, once I've done it, never, ever mention this place to me again.'

CHAPTER SIX

KIT was glad that she had the spring-cleaning job to do in Pimlico. She really needed to be on her own while she returned to equilibrium. She passed on the war poetry, though. It made her cry. So she took some Spanish language tapes with her instead.

By the time the week was over, the house gleamed and Kit knew enough to join a Spanish conversation class.

'At last,' said Tatiana with grudging approval.

Lisa came back from Coral Cove alone. In spite of her tan, she looked peaky.

'Oh, I had another argument with Nikolai,' she said when Kit asked about him. 'He's gone off to watch apes. I don't know where and I don't care.'

'Oh, Lisa, what happened? You seemed so happy together.'

Lisa shrugged, her brightly painted mouth hard. 'That's the way it goes.'

Kit began to be worried. 'What did you argue about this time?'

Lisa shrugged. 'You, as a matter of fact.'

'Me?' Kit could not believe it. 'Why on earth?'

'I take it that Philip Hardesty was Mr First Night?'

Kit flushed.

'Thought so. Well, he wanted your address. Nikolai thinks he's a good guy and was all for giving it to him. I said no.' She spread her scarlet-tipped nails. 'We have lift-off.'

'Oh, no.' Kit was full of remorse. 'I'm so sorry. You shouldn't have to fight about me.'

Lisa gave a deep sigh. 'Hell, Kitten, we're fighting all the time at the moment. If it wasn't about you, it would be about something else. Don't worry about it. Thank God Nikolai has got his apes and I've got a new job. With a bit of luck, if we don't see too much of each other for a while, we'll weather the storm.'

'And if you don't?' asked Kit guiltily.

Lisa lifted her chin. 'Then we're another statistic.' Her voice was steely.

Kit bit her lip.

'Don't look like that,' said Lisa, softening. She gave her sister a quick hug. 'I'm not like Mother. I'll survive just fine.'

After that, by common consent, neither of them talked about Coral Cove again. Even when they met for their monthly Sunday lunch at their mother's home in the country, they both talked hard about the sun, sand and sea. Neither once mentioned a man's name.

'All right,' said Flora Stevens, Kit's god-mother, who was also invited that Sunday. 'Are you going to tell me what happened?'

They were emptying the smart dishwasher that Lisa had bought their mother years earlier and she only ever used when the girls were home. It was Kit's personal theory that her mother did not really know how to use it unaided.

Kit put the large dinner plates into the china cupboard. 'What do you mean?'

'You and Lisa are being so discreet it makes the eardrums twang,' Flora said frankly. 'Even your mother has noticed and that's saying something. Did you have a little waltz round the block with Nikolai?'

'*Flora!*' Kit was genuinely shocked.

'He's an attractive man,' said Flora, unrepentant. 'And with Lisa behaving like a shrew, who could blame him?'

'Me,' said Kit firmly and ungrammatically. But she frowned. 'She is being—well, odd. Isn't she?'

Flora looked wise. 'Maybe,' she said infuriatingly. 'So who was the man you tangled with?'

'You're like the Spanish Inquisition,' said Kit, harassed. 'Does there have to be a man?'

'When you look as if you're on another planet half the time, that's the usual explanation, yes. In your case, you've stopped jumping every time you pass a mirror. I'd say that clinched it.'

Kit stared, not sure whether to laugh or run. In the end she said with feeling, 'The Spanish Inquisition was an understatement.'

Flora stroked the fall of golden hair affectionately. 'All right. I won't ask any more.'

'That's just as well. Because there's nothing to tell.'

Flora looked at her searchingly. 'You all right with this?'

Kit did not pretend to misunderstand. She had a bad history with rejection and Flora was one of the few people apart from Lisa and her mother who knew it.

'I'm not locking myself in my room and refusing to eat, if that's what you're asking,' she said drily.

'I wasn't,' Flora said in a matter-of-fact voice. 'That was an episode and it's over. I know your mother still gets wound up about it, but that's Joanne for you. You said you were over it three years ago and I believe you. But you could still be hurt now. Are you?'

Kit swallowed suddenly. 'Yes.'

Flora nodded. 'And it's hopeless?'

Kit made a clumsy, despairing gesture, more eloquent than words.

'Fair enough,' said Flora, relenting. 'No more questions. But if this hopeless case of yours turns up again, bring him to see me. I'm intrigued by a man who can stop you running away from mirrors.'

Kit pulled a face. But on the way back in Lisa's sports car, she said thoughtfully, 'I think I'd like a mirror for the hall. One of those big Gothic jobs that you see Dracula in.'

Lisa sent her a quick surprised look. But all she said was, 'We can look next weekend.'

They found one in the Portobello street market and had a hysterical Sunday afternoon manhandling it onto the wall, directed by Tatiana.

'This is all wrong, two young girls putting up a great thing like that,' Tatiana scolded. 'Top left corner up half an inch, no more. Yes, it is ridiculous. You need a man.'

As one the sisters said, 'No, we don't.'

And looked at each other and laughed.

Apart from that, though, Kit did not see much of Lisa. The new job took Lisa travelling a lot and Kit was out nearly every night, between her driving lessons and her burgeoning social life.

The Spanish classes had led, somewhat improbably, to a salsa evening. Kit found she liked dancing and she was good at it. Several of the Spanish class signed up for tango lessons.

Two months before, Kit would not have gone. She could not have borne to throw away the multiple layers she used to conceal her body. She would never have dreamed of stripping down to a leotard and swirling skirt.

Now all those old inhibitions seemed stupid. She stopped everyday on her way out to work and looked at herself in the mirror deliberately. Even after her faint tan had faded, she did not look too bad, she thought. Tall, slim, golden hair gleaming with health, wide open grey-green eyes—it could all be a lot worse. After all, everyone else had to look at it. She might as well look too. Sometimes she even applied make-up.

She even enjoyed dancing with partners. Oh, she still didn't date. But she did not freak every time a man put his hands on her any more. These days she knew that physical touch was just that, a brief bridge between person and person.

Of course, there was the touch that hooked your heart out of you on a pin and then stabbed it to the core. But that could presumably not happen twice. So she did not have to worry about that any more.

She took more of an interest in international affairs. She started buying a broadsheet newspaper and turning to the international pages. She even went to the library and surfed the internet.

Lots of sites described the achievements of Philip Hardesty. By contrast Soralaya Khan only got three mentions that Kit could find. She was Brooks Bank's oil expert and had written a learned paper on the movement of international oil prices. She had been interviewed by a satellite news service when one of the Gulf states cut their oil output. And she had been to a ball.

The ball was a charity function. Soralaya was a committee member. That had to be why she merited so many photographs in all the reports, Kit decided. The fact that she looked like a film star was just a bonus.

For Soralaya Khan was a beauty. She was tall and thin as a rail. As a result, her outrageously revealing white lace dress looked striking instead of tarty. In addition to a model girl's figure she had an elaborate pile of lustrous dark hair, a voluptuous scarlet-painted mouth and either perfect skin or the best cosmetics in the universe.

Mind you, she could afford the best cosmetics in the universe, thought Kit. Along with her degrees and her influential ex-boyfriends, more than one society page listed her rich relations. There were plenty of them to list. Soralaya Khan was oil on both sides of the family.

Kit logged off and went home telling herself how glad she was that she had not gone on that alluring honeymoon cruise with Philip Hardesty. Soralaya was not the sort of competition any woman in her right mind could expect to stand up to.

Besides, there had been one photograph—just one—of her with Philip. He had been wearing a dinner jacket and that cool, remote look Kit recognised. Maybe he hadn't been in a very good mood when the photograph was taken, she thought. It didn't make any difference—they were still the perfect couple. Both so tall, so spectacularly good-looking, so *groomed*. Tatiana's black and silver glitter and Lisa's crystal earrings could not begin to make it into that class.

Yes, it was just as well that Kit was not expecting to see Philip Hardesty again. And she wasn't. She *wasn't*.

Winter turned to spring. Kit sniffed the blossom on the trees in the private gardens behind the house and announced to Tatiana that she was thinking of buying some new clothes.

'Better and better,' said Tatiana, her eyes gleaming with missionary fervour. 'A green-eyed blonde ought to be stunning. Do you want company when you go shopping?'

And, laughing, Kit had to admit that she wouldn't mind.

There were only two things that Kit did which were not entirely constructive, Tatiana remarked, on the telephone to Lisa in Zurich. She left the answering machine on all the time, so that she could screen her calls. And she ran to the post every morning with a look of dread. Whatever she dreaded never arrived, clearly. So then she went back down to her flat looking disappointed.

'It is undoubtedly a man,' said Tatiana serenely.

Lisa did not share her complacence. She knew how deep Kit could fall into despair if she was in love and her love was rejected. Not that there was any evidence that she was in love, of course, in spite of what Nikolai said. 'You try to wrap that girl in cotton wool,' he had flung at her in that terminal row. 'But has it ever occurred to you that maybe she needs to work this thing out with Hardesty without the female mafia taking a hand?'

Only Nikolai had not seen Kit sitting on the floor of her bedroom rocking when her tearaway boyfriend had decided she was surplus to requirements.

'Is she—you know—all right?' she asked, wincing at the memory.

'She is more like a twenty-two-year-old than I have ever seen her. A tragic love affair,' said Tatiana largely, 'can be a great source of imaginative stimulus.'

Lisa stopped wincing, snorted with derision and rang off.

Tatiana was hurt. She was pleased with her remark, which had been quite spontaneous. So she repeated it to Kit when they set out on their shopping expedition.

Kit stared at her for a full thirty seconds before saying, 'Gee, thanks. You're a great comfort.'

Tatiana was not good at picking up irony. 'Women should always have some experience of heartbreak. It gives them mystery.'

Kit exploded into laughter. 'Come along, you old mountebank. I'm not playing the Lady of Camellias. I just want some summer clothes.'

Tatiana was curious. 'Are you saying your heart is *not* broken?'

If she had learned one thing from deceptive Philip Hardesty it was the use of evasion, thought Kit. When Tatiana had tried to grill her before she went to Coral Cove, Kit had either run away or got hopelessly flustered.

Now she just said calmly, 'Broken or not, my heart is no concern of yours, Tatiana.'

The older woman looked delighted. 'I look forward to meeting him.'

Even that did not draw Kit. 'Nice try,' she said ironically. 'Now leave it alone. Or I'll go shopping on my own.'

'No, no. You will get terrible colours and skirts to your ankles,' said Tatiana with some justice, based on the evidence. 'I will come. And we will not speak of this mystery lover until you want to.'

Philip sat quietly in the comfortable armchair and waited for the verdict. The specialist had the best reputation in New York. But Philip did not expect good news.

The ophthalmologist sat down on the corner of his desk and drummed with his pen on the file he had been studying.

'Well?' said Philip. 'Don't be afraid to tell me. I can deal with it, whatever it is.'

The ophthalmologist nodded. 'Yeah,' he said absently. 'If I knew what to tell you.' He sucked his teeth. 'Truth is—this is a real puzzle. I'll be honest, Sir Philip. I don't know what's going on here.'

Philip frowned. This sounded like honesty, not some unnecessary softening to let the patient down lightly. 'What do you mean?'

'This occasional blindness in your left eye. I can see it. I know it's happening. It's not psychosomatic. I can track it. But—there's no physical reason for it.'

'What?' It was the last thing Philip had expected.

'It comes at random. That's unusual. No obvious signals, either before or during the episode. You said that no one else has even noticed?'

'That's right.'

'You see, that's even more unusual.' The doctor folded his arms. 'Best explanation I can give you, right? It's as if your eye is shutting down. It needs to rest, so it rests. It just stops seeing.'

Philip considered. 'That doesn't sound likely.'

The doctor grinned. 'You're right. It's crazy. But—not impossible. Very rare but not unheard of. I've turned up a couple of dozen cases worldwide.'

Philip digested this. 'So, what's the prognosis?'

'Depends what the underlying cause is. If it's stress, there's a good chance you'll get your sight back in full. As long as you stop doing whatever it is that's causing the stress, of course.'

He encountered Philip's cool displeasure and his grin widened.

'Like my job?' asked Philip politely.

'Hey, you said it, not me.'

Philip looked down his nose. 'It is such an easy target.'

The doctor got off the corner of his desk. 'Up to you. You do what you want. There's no procedure and no medication. I wouldn't be doing my job if I told you different.'

Philip had to acknowledge the truth of that. He shifted in the chair and said ruefully, 'Sorry. I ought to know about telling people truths they don't want to hear.' He gave his sudden, glinting smile. 'It's part of my job too.'

The doctor softened to that smile the way everyone did. Or everyone but Kit Romaine, thought Philip. The elusive Kit Romaine, on whom three separate lines of enquiry had drawn a blank so far.

'Look, it's none of my business. But you've obviously been pushing yourself for years. Why don't you just let up a bit?'

Philip sighed. 'Live for today?' he said drily. 'Somebody was telling me to do just that only recently.'

The doctor shrugged. 'You could try it.'

Philip laughed suddenly. 'Only if I have a character transplant.'

'Then there's nothing else I can think of. Carry on like this and my guess is, it will get worse.'

'Thank you,' said Philip. He stood up and shook hands.

But he was still smiling when he walked out of the building.

Live for today. Was it possible?

Maybe it was, if he found his unicorn girl again. But so far his assistant's researches had turned up nothing. And he had not had time to look for himself.

What if he did that now? What if he went back to his desk and did not give up until he found her? Would she even want to see him again? And if not, could he persuade her?

He contemplated the prospect. His mouth curled with sheer delight at the picture it conjured up. *Could* he?

An hour later he was quietly furious.

'You have not even tried,' he said to Fernando.

'I found the brother-in-law,' said the assistant defensively. 'I even sent him a fax.'

'And look—' Philip gestured at the file. 'He's up-country, watching gorillas. Your fax will either go straight into a waste-paper basket somewhere. Or it will take months to reach him. You didn't *think.*'

'It's not my job to keep track of your girl-friends,' Fernando muttered.

Philip stiffened. 'No,' he said evenly. 'You're right. It isn't. But if you objected you should have said so. If you didn't you should have shown more initiative. Now get out.'

Fernando did. He was shaken. Philip had never turned his famous displeasure on him before.

Fernando felt as if he had been dunked in the Arctic. And all for a girl he had not even known Philip was interested in!

What, thought Fernando, would Soralaya say about that?

It was a long time since Philip had done his own research. He found he soon got back into the swing of it. You go down one line of enquiry, he thought, and when that ran out you went down another. You just had to keep checking back with the first line of results all the time.

If he couldn't get in touch with the brother-in-law he would see if he could find the sister. She had not been helpful at Coral Cove but at least she wasn't sitting in the jungle, watching primates with her husband. He found the expedition's personnel lists on the internet.

An hour later he sat back, looking thoughtful. So Countess Lisa Ivanov was Lisa Romaine, newly appointed global bond strategist. Now, was he going to call her, out of the blue, and ask her for Kit's address again? Or was he going to go to work in a more roundabout way?

It just depended what his contacts in the banking world could come up with. He smiled and picked up the phone.

'Soralaya? Good to hear you. Look, I need a favour. Who do you know in London?'

*   *   *

Kit always enjoyed herself at Henderson's book shop. It was a crowded, lively place, with every corner and table piled with books, rare and popular, new and secondhand. The shelving system was of the roughest, because books came and went so fast through Alan Henderson's hands. But all the assistants knew exactly where to find any book.

Kit, as they often told her, was the only temporary member of staff they had ever had who managed to do the same.

'How's the self-improvement programme?' Alan asked when she reported for work the first Monday morning.

'I'm doing south-east Asian birds at the moment,' said Kit.

She did not wholly want to forget Coral Cove, she found, even though she did not want to talk about it. So she had a project to identify some of the birds she had seen there. Some of the *other* birds. The ones her compulsive labeller had not given her the names of already.

Alan raised his eyebrows. 'Inspired by the brother-in-law, eh? So you'll be going to the Rainforest Ball, of course?'

Kit was alarmed. 'Hey, I'm just reading a few books. I've not joined the charity set yet.'

Alan grinned. 'If you don't support it there'll be no rainforest left in a hundred years. You'd better come as my partner.'

Kit was indignant. 'That's moral blackmail.'

'Yup,' he said cheerfully. 'It's on the last Saturday you're with us this time. It can be your farewell present.'

She glowered. But between her new confidence, her new clothes and her tango lessons, she gave in eventually. She was even quite excited by the idea, although she did not say so.

'Say, thank you very much, Alan, I'd love to come with you, you've swept me off my feet,' said Alan, bubbling over.

'You couldn't sweep me off my feet with a supermarket trolley,' said Kit frankly.

Alan was a seventy-year-old faun who came up to her shoulder. He laughed and agreed.

None of that made any difference. Tatiana announced that it was absolutely essential that Kit have a full-length ball dress.

'Isn't that a bit old-fashioned?' said Kit. She did not know much about charity balls but she was no fool.

'Alan Henderson is old-fashioned,' said Tatiana superbly. 'We will look at the weekend.'

Kit puffed but in the end she agreed. Secretly she was rather excited about having a ball dress. The only time she had really dressed up in living memory was when she had worn Tatiana's borrowed finery at Coral Cove. It would be nice to see how she could look if she set about the enterprise properly. Within a reasonable budget, of course.

So on Sunday Tatiana took her on a tour of her favourite thrift shops.

It was not a success. Tatiana liked to flit from shop to shop; to go back to one and try a scarf or a handbag she had seen in one with a skirt she had seen in another. Given her choice, she would have had Kit in and out of outfits like a Barbie doll. Kit was beginning to wonder whether she should just march Tatiana home and start off again on her own, when a flash of iridescent blue in a tumble of black skirts caught her eye.

'What's that?'

'Not blue,' said Tatiana categorically. 'Blondes always think they can wear blue and they can't.'

But Kit was not taking any notice. She was scrabbling through the pile of creased stuff with the first enthusiasm she had shown all day.

When she pulled it out it was ragged, a black sateen under-dress with a sweep of butterfly beading in purple and lilac; lapis lazuli, aquamarine and jade; all stitched onto net that was so flimsy it was falling apart.

'Oh, it's in holes,' Kit said, disappointed.

But Tatiana pushed her out of the way.

'That can be fixed. You have a better eye than I thought,' she said. She held it up against Kit, her lips pursed. 'Ye-es. Dramatic. You're coming out of your shell, aren't you? We'll take it.'

Kit's doubts were reinforced by the nice volunteer who was manning the till. The woman looked so dubious when Tatiana waved the dress at her that Kit muttered in her ear, 'Leave it. It was a nice idea. But the thing is falling apart.'

Tatiana chose not to hear.

'All right,' said Kit on the way home. 'We've got a dress for the price of a packet of dusters. That's good. Only I won't be able to wear it. It's so old, it's indecent. So I'll have to go looking for something else next week. I can't go before my driving test on Tuesday and the dance is on Saturday.' Her voice began to climb in panic.

Tatiana was unimpressed. 'There's a lot of work to do, that's all. I am going to introduce you to the crochet hook.'

She did. In the end Kit was so fascinated by the intricate knotting and stitching that the dress required that she actually began to enjoy it. For the first time she put on a dress and actually wanted to look at it in the mirror. By Saturday it was a work of art. And she had passed her driving test too.

'Licensed to drive. Licensed to knock 'em dead,' said Kit, turning this way and that in front of her Dracula mirror.

What would Philip Hardesty have said to *this*? Not, Let my colleague escort you back to your cottage, you poor, sensitive little shrimp, that's for certain, thought Kit, baring her teeth at her reflection.

'No jewellery, said Tatiana, surveying her professionally. 'That dress is all the jewellery you need. But you will need to do something with your hair. Will you let me put it up?'

Kit was too enchanted with herself to demur. She preened. The dress was the simplest possible shape, sleeveless and low-necked. Yet somehow the glittering colours made it look as if her body was impossibly slim and lithe under it, as graceful as a dragonfly.

Or an Asian fairy bluebird, thought Kit, stroking the cobalt iridescence with gentle fingers. She had not told Tatiana why she had seized upon the dress. That was still her secret, along with Philip Hardesty.

But when she looked at herself in the mirror before Alan arrived to collect her she found herself wishing with all her heart that Philip could see her like this. With her corn-gold hair looped into a series of soft and complicated swirls and her lips painted an enticing cerise, she looked like an exotic creature. Not any longer the naïve idiot he had encountered on Coral Cove. Would he be able to resist her now?

Well, she was never going to find out. Kit told herself she was glad she was not going to. But Alan's reaction was nevertheless balm to the soul.

'Wow,' he said reverently. 'I'm going to be with the hottest babe at the party.'

And Kit, who winced and blushed and fled when anyone paid her a compliment on her looks, laughed with delight.

'I'm beginning to know how Cinderella felt,' she said. 'Let's go.'

Philip nearly didn't go to the ball. He had only arrived in London the day before and he had to go down to his country house the next day. There were things that he had put off too long, that had to be done before he could turn his attention to the hunt for the unicorn.

He rented a car for the next day and then tried all the contacts he had thought would help him find Kit. He drew a blank. Lisa Romaine was travelling, probably somewhere in Switzerland. Nobody knew her sister.

He did not even know which telephone book to scan. After all, there was no evidence that she lived in London. His Kit did not feel like a city swinger. He gave a tender smile but it soon died.

He had flung himself back on the bed in the luxury hotel room he hardly noticed, hands behind his head. Then one of the friends of friends of friends rang back.

'Look, Sir Philip, there's the Rainforest Ball tonight. The Ivanovs are great supporters. They would be there if they were in London. Anyway, lots of people who know them really well will certainly come. Maybe someone will know an address for the sister-in-law. We've taken a table. You could join our party, if you liked.'

Philip's heart sank. He did his share of charity dances and private views in New York and they were not his idea of a good time. But the man was so transparently trying to be helpful. And Philip was fresh out of other ideas.

So in the end he said 'Yes' and looked forward gloomily to a boring evening.

First of all, to his annoyance, he had to hire a dinner jacket. He had not brought his own. It had not occurred to him that he would need it. Anyway, he had packed so fast when he decided to go to London to look for her that he had brought the bare minimum. It would be lucky if the dinner jacket was the only thing he had to supply himself with, thought Philip ironically.

He did not recognise himself in this impulsive man. Normally he planned to a fault. Whenever he travelled he had a comprehensive list of every last thing he had ever needed. Yet here he was in the most expensive hotel in London with one carry-on case.

His mouth lifted in a wry smile. Living for today was obviously going to be more of a challenge than he had bargained for.

At first the dance fulfilled all his bleakest expectations. The bankers were pleasant but he did not know any of them. They welcomed him but they did not know what to talk to him about and ended up asking him about his work. Philip began to feel he was back on duty.

And then he looked up. And saw her.

Saw her.

He went cold.

It had never occurred to him that Kit would be here. It was the last place he would have expected to see her, his shy unicorn girl. He thought of her alone and free. In his imagination she ran through forest paths. Or played unselfconsciously in the water.

She did not dance, laughing, in the middle of a jewelled and artificial crowd. Philip could not take his eyes off her. Nor could half the other men in the room. He had not bargained on that either.

She looked—different. Exotic, somehow. Still vivid with life and pleasure but with a secret there. Surely the secret was new, he thought. There had not been that reserve in her eyes when he held her in his arms on Coral Cove.

His body stirred at the memory.

She was dancing as unselfconsciously as she swam. Under the gleaming dress her body was never still. She was supple as water. Philip felt sweat break out on the back of his neck.

She was laughing at something her partner was saying. And yet there was something about her that looked so alone. Alone and heartbreakingly sexy.

Hardly knowing that he was moving, Philip got to his feet.

'Thank you,' said his neighbour, misunderstanding. 'I'd love to dance.'

Philip jumped and looked down. She gave him a polite smile and stood up. She was so plainly doing her duty that he laughed in spite of himself. He held out his hand.

'Excellent. Maybe you can very kindly tell me who all these people are.'

'I don't know many,' she demurred.

But it turned out that she knew the older man who was making Kit laugh so uninhibitedly.

'Alan Henderson. Owns one of the best independent book shops in London. Don't know the girl. She's beautiful, isn't she?'

'Yes,' said Philip proudly.

When their dance was over he went out to the lobby and scanned the seating plan. Kit was sitting at a publishers' table. It looked as if she had come with Mr Henderson.

Well, that was all right, Philip told himself. She loved books. She had even wanted to be a librarian, for heaven's sake. Maybe this was professional networking, though it did not seem like her. But she could not be interested in Alan Henderson in any other way, of course.

She could not be interested in any other man. Of course she could not. She was *his*.

He began to prowl the rooms restlessly, seeking her.

Kit would not have believed that a big formal dance like this could be so much fun. Everyone had been so nice to her. The women had admired her dress, envied her hair aloud. The men had plied her with champagne and queued up to dance with her. She was on top of the world.

In fact, she should be perfectly happy. She would have been perfectly happy. If only she could stop thinking about Coral Cove and the tropical night when Philip Hardesty had not admired any damn thing about her at all. He couldn't have done. Or he would not have found it so easy to leave her.

And then the voice from her dreams said roughly in her ear, 'Come and dance with me.'

Kit froze. Then she swung round, staring.

He was here.

He was *here*.

He put his hands on her bare arms and it was like walking into a force field. She gasped.

'You look wonderful.' He didn't sound pleased about it for some reason.

Kit found her voice. 'What are you doing here?'

'Looking for you.'

'What?'

He did not answer. 'Dance with me,' he said again.

It was heaven to see him.

No, it wasn't, it was terrifying. He looked so distinguished in his formal black clothes, with his crisp shirt gleaming and his black tie in an expert bow. Not only distinguished but effortlessly in command. He was at home among these sorts of people. He had probably been tying bow ties since he was six. He must be able to see instantly that she did not belong here in her ragbag dress.

She said the first thing that came into her head. 'I don't dance.'

'Yes, you do. I've seen you. Not very good for my blood pressure, either.'

'Oh, with Alan!'

The dark eyes lifted at her tone. 'Alan doesn't count?'

Kit flushed. 'That's a horrible thing to say.'

But there was a look of quiet triumph about Philip. 'Alan doesn't count,' he said, nodding with satisfaction. 'So you can risk being in his arms but not in mine.'

It was not a question. Kit flushed harder.

'Dance with me, Kit,' he said softly.

Against all her resolutions—against all of her instincts but one—she did.

When they got onto the dance floor the band had switched to the slow, smoochy stuff. *Help,* thought Kit.

Philip put his arms round her and drew her close. But not too close. They kept time to the whispering music, moving as if they were in a dream. He held her loosely, his cheek against her hair.

Kit thought, *He wants me now because he's got some free time on his hands. It's convenient. If only he wanted me when it wasn't convenient.*

She thought her heart would break.

Which was crazy. Because Philip Hardesty was nothing to do with her and never would be. Never could be.

As if to turn all her certainties on her head, he murmured into her hair, 'Do you know how hard you are to find?'

Kit swallowed. There was no answer to that. Or not one that she wanted to risk.

He held her a little away from him and looked down at her. 'Didn't you wonder why I hadn't been in touch?'

'No,' said Kit, lying hard.

'I knew so little about you. I didn't know where to start. And then the only links I had to you, your family, had to take off round the world.'

'You've been in touch with Lisa?' said Kit with foreboding. After her sister had fallen out with her husband in order to protect Kit's privacy! How would she take that? And what on earth would Kit say when Lisa phoned, demanding an explanation? As she inevitably would.

He shook his head. 'Not since she first refused to tell me how to get in touch with you on Coral Cove. She moves too fast. Every time I thought I'd caught up with her she'd moved on. It was very frustrating.'

Kit pulled herself together. 'She wouldn't have told you anything anyway. She would have got in touch with me first. And I would have said—'

'Yes?'

'I'd have said, tell him nothing,' announced Kit firmly. She was trying to convince herself as much as him. Maybe more.

He pulled her back into his arms with a soft laugh. 'Sure you would.'

She leaned back against his arm, looking up at him through narrowed eyes. They were jade in the artificial lights glinting up from her dress.

'You're very sure of yourself, aren't you?'

Philip shook his head. 'Not for a minute. But I know something special when I see it.' He paused before adding softly, 'And I think you do too.'

Kit's mouth dried.

'Stop it,' she said loudly. 'Stop—stop purring at me like that. I told you—'

Philip's arms tightened. 'You told me never to use the word love to you again,' he said quietly. 'So how else do you want me to put it?'

Kit felt hot all over. She looked round, acutely self-conscious. But no one was listening to their conversation. No one was even looking at them.

She still said, 'You're embarrassing me.'

'Fine,' said Philip obligingly.

Before she knew what he was doing he had loosed his arms, seized her unready hand, and tugged her off the dance floor.

'What are you *doing*?' said Kit, stumbling after him.

'Finding somewhere we can talk. Without *embarrassing* you.'

He pulled her out into the lobby. There was an elevator with its doors open. Philip pulled her inside and punched the button for the basement.

'Right,' he said. 'No audience, unless you count the security cameras.'

The elevator hit the basement. The doors opened soundlessly. Philip pressed a button to keep them locked that way.

'Another skill I learned from my father's troop,' he said, pleased with himself. 'Now, where was I?'

'Purring,' said Kit involuntarily. She caught herself. 'Now, look. You can't just highjack my life here. Come to that, you can't drag me away from my friends—'

Philip ignored that. 'There was something between us,' he said intensely. 'It was the worst possible timing. And I probably didn't handle it all that well. But there was something. At least admit it.'

There was a small pause. Kit's heart started to pound so loudly he must surely hear it. She could not bear it. She turned her shoulder, as if she was impatient to be gone.

'That's nonsense. You can't seriously stand there and say that you're in love with me. Not—'

'I'm not saying that.'

Kit was disconcerted and rather put out. 'Well, then—'

She reached for the elevator control panel. There had to be a button to press to release those doors.

Philip caught her hand and swung her round to face him. He said flatly, 'I don't know what love means.'

That brought Kit's head up with a vengeance.

'Oh, great! Just great! So I'm signed up to give you a crash course, I suppose?'

Philip looked startled. Then, from nowhere, deeply amused.

'I hadn't thought of that. But it's certainly an idea.'

Kit was so angry she could barely speak. 'Forget it.'

She tugged at her hand. He would not release it. He was a lot stronger than she expected. Than she remembered. Though, now she thought about it—

'Let me *go*,' yelled Kit, suddenly hot.

He didn't.

He said, 'What I mean is—this is new to me. I haven't felt like this before.'

She was still glaring at him. He tried his best smile, the warm one that started slowly. It worked on despots and delinquents alike. Only of course, now he remembered, on Kit it had no effect whatsoever.

'You jerked me around on Coral Cove,' she said in a voice that shook with suppressed rage. At least she hoped it was rage. 'And now you're trying to do it again. Well, not to me, you don't, buster.'

She dragged her hand out of his grasp at last and dived for freedom across the basement. It was a car park. Her footsteps rang on the concrete as if she were wearing tap shoes.

He caught her as she was hauling open the door to the emergency stairs. He had stopped smiling and his hair—his immaculate raven hair—was dishevelled. Even his bow tie seemed to be off true centre at last.

'Kit, listen to me, please.' His voice was urgent. More than urgent. Frantic. 'I'm going down to the country tomorrow. Come with me. Talk to me. We can't just—'

She spun round, too furious to be rational.

'Don't tell me what I can and can't do!'

The shutter slammed down on his left eye without warning. Philip staggered, shocked.

'And I've *talked* to you. You were the one who wasn't talking, if you remember? *Sir* Philip! Mr Peace! Big cheese pretending to be little cheese so he could—' She stopped. 'What's wrong?' she said in quite a different voice.

Philip put his hand against the wall to steady himself. Kit flinched at the sudden movement. He did not notice.

He shook his head, as if he was trying to clear it. 'I—'

She stepped back to him. He seemed unaware of that too, she thought. He put a hand up to his forehead.

'Are you hurt?'

'No. It's nothing.' He was trying to pull himself together. She could see that something had shaken him badly.

She put a hand on his left arm. 'Look, I didn't mean—'

He swung round to face her. He didn't just turn his head, he turned his whole body. It was a clumsy movement. Philip Hardesty, who was even graceful when he was confronting hostile guerrillas, made a *clumsy* movement. She had only seen him make an uncontrolled movement like that once before. When he had nearly dropped that glass at the reception. And looked round to see if anyone had noticed.

She put up a hand and turned his face towards her gently. When she saw his expression, his face was naked.

Kit said on a long note of discovery, 'You can't *see*!'

CHAPTER SEVEN

PHILIP gave a crack of laughter. 'Do you know you're the first person to say that? It's been happening for months and nobody's noticed. I live surrounded by people and not one of them saw that very often I couldn't make one eye work.'

Kit was silent for a minute. 'How bad is it?'

He shrugged.

She took a decision. 'All right. We'll talk. Just talk. But not in a car park. We'll go upstairs and find some coffee and you can tell me about it.'

It was not, thought Philip, the sweeping off her feet that he had planned. But at least it was better than her running for cover and swearing never to see him again. Besides, he was feeling shaky. The shutter had never come down with such savage suddenness before.

It cleared as they went back upstairs. With the returning sight, an idea occurred to Philip.

She had been sympathetic. Well, relatively. It was not ideal. But his training taught him to use whatever came to hand. Maybe his loss of eyesight was the tool to get Kit to give him a hearing.

He pulled a face. He did not like it. Not his style at all. Normally he ignored all signs of physical weakness in himself. The idea of making a big production of this one was distasteful.

But she was so adamant, even now. And you had to roll with the punches. He wasn't going to tell any lies, he promised himself. But maybe he might exaggerate a little the extent to which he was no longer in control of his body.

Salutary, thought Philip with wry self-mockery. He had been in control of everything for longer than he cared to remember. Now his unicorn girl was forcing him back into a position of uncertainty again. It was going to be an interesting learning experience!

They avoided the ballroom and went instead to the hotel bar. It was all shining mahogany and muted music. People came and went all the time. Businessmen waited for clients. Hotel guests returned from an evening out. Families reunited. Lone travellers sat sipping at a nightcap before they turned in.

It could not have been more anonymous. Not a soul took any notice of them, once the barman had brought them coffee.

'Tell,' Kit commanded.

Philip hesitated for a minute. Then he shrugged and gave her a severely truncated rundown of the specialist's opinion.

'Not very interesting,' he concluded dismis-
sively. 'Nothing to be done.'

He had not told her about the ophthalmologist's advice to live for today.

She looked at him narrowly. 'Is that true?'

Philip bit back a smile. 'No one else in my life
would have asked me that.'

'Why? Have you negotiated them all into sub-
mission?' said Kit sourly.

'I suppose I have,' he said without rancour.

He sat back in the leather armchair, watching
the play of expression over her face. He had
never seen her with make-up on before. With her
mouth voluptuously red, she suddenly seemed
less youthful, more determined. Or maybe her
character had changed since Coral Cove. She
must have had the fright of her life when Rafek
swaggered out of the night to challenge him.
Perhaps it had changed her.

'So you're not going to take anybody's advice,' she diagnosed.

'Nobody has offered me any,' he said mildly.

Kit snorted. 'Have you asked for any?'

He was fascinated by the way her eyes
changed colour, now jade, now emerald, now
sea-grey. He leaned forward.

'I don't think you understand what my life is
like. I work. I travel eighty per cent of the time.
I see my friends twice a year if I'm lucky. I live

alone. Who do I ask for advice? My assistant? The janitor in my building?'

Kit was appalled by the bleak picture he conjured up. She almost softened.

Then she remembered that article. And her internet researches on Soralaya Khan, daughter of oil magnates, supporter of fashionable charities. Philip Hardesty was doing what he did best—manipulating her sympathies.

So she said drily, 'Oh, I'm sure you've forgotten someone. There must be the odd girlfriend in there somewhere.'

'Oh, girlfriends,' said Philip in the tone in which he might have said, 'Oh, chocolate truffles!'

They were nice but not important, Kit deduced. And in plentiful supply.

She stood up, the lapis-lazuli dress glinting like underwater treasures.

Ever the gentleman, Philip got to his feet.

How tall he was. How handsome in his dinner jacket, with his midnight hair and sculpted profile. And that air of contained intensity.

Kit avoided his eyes.

'Talk to one of those girlfriends of yours,' she suggested crisply. 'You might even try treating her with respect. And then take her advice.'

She swept off without a backward look.

Philip looked after her with dudgeon. That was not supposed to happen. He had played the noble, suffering card rather well, he thought. And she had positively refused to be moved by it. It left him feeling bruised and rather a fool.

What did she mean, try treating a girlfriend with respect? He always treated women with respect. He prided himself on it. He—

Philip stopped his thoughts dead, almost with astonishment. She had really got under his skin, hadn't she? He had never sat fulminating like this after other women left him. She had weapons, his unicorn girl, and she knew where to aim them.

This was interesting. This was more than interesting, this was unique. Of course, he had known that before. But this was a new aspect of Kit Romaine. It would need careful consideration. And even more careful handling.

Thoughtfully, he went back to the ballroom.

Well, it had happened, thought Kit. She had said goodnight to Alan, given Tatiana an edited account of her evening and now she was alone in her flat. She did not turn on the light. She stood in front of her Dracula mirror, looking at her shadowed reflection in the sodium light that filtered in from the street.

She almost did not recognise herself. The light drained all the colour from dress and hair. She was all graceful draperies and pale limbs, like the water nymph he had once called her. In the darkness she saw with a little shock that her mouth was richly, sensuously curved. Why had she never realised that before? And her eyes glittered.

Alive. That was what she looked. *Alive.*

He had found her at last. She had waited for it, dreaded it, dreaded it not happening, *ached* for him, ashamed of the ache. And now it was done and he was here and she had sent him away. Sent him away, when just the thought of him made her eyes glitter like diamonds and her lips part in anticipation.

'I must be out of my mind,' groaned Kit.

She would have to find him. She could not leave it like that, she knew. No matter what it cost her. He was right. There was something between them. The girl in the lapis-lazuli dress acknowledged it with every shimmering pulse.

There was a question. It had been asked that night under the stars. He might not have made love to her. But she had offered him her heart on a pin. She knew that now. There was nothing she could do to call it back. She had to go on to the end of the road—or stay in the limbo of 'what if?' for the rest of her life.

'All right,' she told her reflection. 'You win. Heaven help me.'

Philip had gone to work with all the care of his professional training. If any one of his fellow guests had been asked the next day, they would have said with complete conviction that he had not asked about Kit Romaine. More, that he had not shown any interest in her.

But he worked the tables, bringing the conversation round time and again towards the girl in the bluebird dress. Kit would have been surprised at how much people knew about her. Philip, committing every chance remark to memory, was not. Kit Romaine was memorable at all times. But last night she had been stunning, like quicksilver incarnate.

He ended up with a fair picture of her life, her friends and her habits. There was only one thing he did not get. Her address.

He rang the land agent at Ashbarrow and told him that he was postponing his visit indefinitely.

'But there are some serious decisions we have to talk about,' said Geoffrey Bass, alarmed.

'Have to wait,' said Philip, kind but immoveable. 'I've got to stay in London to do something important.'

Geoffrey regarded Philip's job with respect bordering on awe. He accepted the excuse immediately. 'Important talks?'

'Crucial,' said Philip with feeling.

As soon as he rang off he went straight back to the arduous task of finding where Kit Romaine lived.

Kit felt more and more uncertain as she sat in the rattling underground train. The Sunday-morning crowd was full of cheerful tourists. Parents were taking children to museums. Families were going shopping. Lovers were on their way to family visits when they would rather still be in bed together.

It was all so normal. She felt like the only freak. Though maybe that was because she was shaking inside the whole time.

She felt even more of a freak when she walked into Philip's hotel. She had thought that the venue for last night's ball was grand. But it was nothing compared to this place. Half-hidden in an elegant mews, the front door looked like a private house, albeit a grand one. Once inside, she found herself surrounded by leather and chintz and oak-panelled walls hung with sporting prints and Victorian portraits. It was hard to work out which of the polished tables constituted the reception desk.

Kit hovered in the entrance. Her cotton trousers and chain-store jacket had felt smart enough when she left home. But here they looked what they were—clumsily tailored and poor quality. She felt hopelessly outclassed. Her shaking increased.

One of the hotel staff took pity on her.

'Can I help you, miss?'

Kit swallowed. 'I want to see Philip Hardesty,' she announced in a high, tight voice.

Alan had found his hotel for her. She did not know how. Rather contrary to her expectations, the desk clerk or whatever he was did not glare at her suspiciously.

'Sir Philip?'

Sir! Of course! She'd forgotten that. No wonder she was feeling outclassed.

'Let me just check whether he is staying with us,' said the desk clerk discreetly. 'Your name, miss?'

She told him. He went, presumably to sound out the honoured guest about whether he wanted to acknowledge the downmarket article asking for him in the lobby. Kit walked to the log fire and spread her fingers to the blaze. It made no difference. It did not seem that anything could warm her.

And then a voice behind her said incredulously, 'Kit?'

And she was fiery hot.

He took her hand. She did not resist. He looked round the cosy lobby, so like a private house, and said in a harassed voice, 'We can't talk here. I won't ask you up to my room. But what about a walk?'

'Fine,' said Kit. She felt numb but at least the blush was subsiding.

He walked her through streets of overpoweringly tall buildings, past a palace or two and through the gates of St James's Park. Kit drew a steadying breath.

The trees were coming into bright green leaf. A thin sunshine drizzled their tops with honey. From the bridge over the lake, the offices of Whitehall looked like a sultan's palace of turrets between the willows.

'This is so beautiful,' she said involuntarily.

'I've always liked it,' agreed Philip. 'Now tell me.'

Kit did not pretend to misunderstand him. She said with difficulty, 'I wish I'd not said those things last night.'

'Ah.'

'Not that they were wrong,' she said quickly. 'I stand by every word. But there were other things to say, you were right about that. I should have stuck around and talked.'

Philip nodded.

'Say something,' said Kit, goaded.

'I was thinking.'

'Oh, hell.'

That startled him. 'What?'

'Whenever you start to think you end up trying to pull my strings,' said Kit frankly. 'I hate it.'

He thought about his cynical ploy to engage her sympathy using his erratic eyesight. Philip was suddenly burningly ashamed of himself.

'Ah.'

Kit did a little tap dance of frustration. 'There you go again. Why don't you just say what you mean? I can't take all this calculation and weighing and phony diplomacy. It's not human.'

Philip was taken aback. 'Live for today?' he said, struggling to find it amusing. But he was shaken by her vehemence.

'You could do worse.'

He took a deep breath. 'All right. Talk to one of my girlfriends. Treat her with respect. Listen to her advice,' he said as if he was repeating a lesson. 'Come with me to my home.'

'*What?*'

He looked away with a little laugh. 'Don't like it, do you? That was me saying what I mean without diplomacy.'

Kit turned to face him. Her eyes were green as the spring this morning, he thought. And very serious.

'You want me to come away with you? Why?'

He spread his hands. 'To talk. To be together. I've got to go anyway. There's so much to do and I've neglected it for months. It would be the ideal opportunity to show you who I am. To see—'

He broke off, slamming a fist into the palm of his other hand. It was an uncharacteristic gesture, uncontrolled and almost violent. She watched it without comment.

'Oh, this is stupid. Why would you go away with me? Even if I were the right age for you, you and I have nothing in common. As it is, I'm an old bore who can't see straight.'

He had not been referring to his eyesight but she said swiftly, 'Are you driving home?'

'What?' He was disconcerted. It took him a moment to understand the practical question she was asking. 'Oh, yes, I've arranged to pick up a car today. If I go.'

She said coolly, 'Should you be driving with one eye unreliable?'

He had not thought of that. He had not been thinking of anything but her for days now, it seemed.

'Oh, damn,' he said as the reason for her question hit him.

She said clearly, 'You need a back-up driver.'

Philip stared.

Kit smiled. She had stopped shaking at last, she realised.

'I won't come with you as a stand-in mistress,' she told him clearly.

'*Kit!*'

'But I will come as a co-driver and temporary assistant. You'll have a proper contract with my employer and you'll keep your hands off me. And we'll talk.'

Philip looked at her for a long moment. Then a light began to gleam in his eyes.

'You drive a hard bargain.'

Kit lifted her chin.

'Take it or leave it.'

'I'll take it,' said Philip hastily. 'Believe me, I'll take whatever I can get.'

She held him to their bargain. A bemused Helen Ludwig completed the contract form and pushed it across the desk. Philip signed without reading it. He looked at Kit, his eyes full of affectionate amusement.

'Satisfied?'

'I feel reasonably in control now,' she agreed serenely.

Secretly she was hugging herself. No more Miss Wimp who was too sensitive for her own good, she thought. This was Kit Romaine, asserting herself. And proving she could take on the best and win!

It was a long drive. He offered her the chance to take the wheel but Kit was gracious about refusing. She was not about to tell him that she had held a driving licence for less than a week. She knew she was a good driver but she lacked experience, especially of driving with a passenger who had haunted her dreams for months. She did not want her first shunt to be in a hired limousine either.

So she said firmly, 'I'm the back-up. If your eyes give you trouble, I'll take over. Otherwise you're on your own.'

'Very decisive,' he murmured, his lips twitching.

It was a long, long journey. And not just in the miles they covered to his Devon mansion.

'How did you get into the peace-negotiation business?' asked Kit.

'By accident. International service was a compromise. My father was a soldier. Our whole family were. Dad wanted me to follow him into the Brigade. But my mother hated the idea. When he was away she used to go mad, expecting to hear that he'd been killed. When he was home she spent her whole time waiting for him to be posted again.'

'Sounds like a great marriage,' said Kit drily.

'It had its moments,' agreed Philip.

'They're still together?'

'Dead,' he said. 'Accident, five years ago. That's when Ashbarrow started on the slide. I hadn't expected to inherit so soon. And I just haven't had the time to get to grips with it.'

He sounded so cool. Kit hesitated, then said carefully, 'Do you still miss them?'

Philip looked surprised. 'You must understand, I never saw that much of them. I was at school, they were abroad. I saw more of my grandparents. My grandfather was always saying I couldn't expect to absorb my parents' time. They had higher duties. He was strong on duty, my grandfather.' He smiled reminiscently.

Not a hint of bitterness, thought Kit, amazed. She gave a little shiver. 'Sounds grim.'

'Does it?' He was surprised. 'But I had so many privileges. If you're given a lot, you owe a lot.'

Kit found her throat was tight for some reason. 'Not your whole life,' she said disagreeably.

She wanted to put her arms round him and cradle his head against her breast. Crazy. When he was not asking for sympathy. And was driving, to boot!

He was unaware. 'No,' he said ruefully. 'I was the one who put my whole life into my job. Sheer vanity, I'm afraid. I like to be the best.'

'Yes,' said Kit, she could see that.

He glanced at her sideways. 'So goodbye to the private life. The technical expression is crowded out.'

She nearly asked about Soralaya Khan. So nearly. But he was talking about his job and the moment passed.

'And, of course, the professional scepticism did not help.'

She did not understand. 'Professional?' she echoed, puzzled.

'Taking the heat out of dramatic feelings. That's what I do for a living. Never respond in anger. Never react. That's a killer when it comes to personal relationships.'

Kit could not believe it. 'You're never angry?'

He shrugged. 'Can't afford it. Besides, it might just tip the scales if someone was thinking of coming after me.'

'Coming after you?' Kit realised what he was talking about with horror. 'Are you a target, then?'

'Let's say I could be a useful bargaining counter,' Philip said levelly. He was putting the car through the leafy lanes of England in spring as if they were in a time capsule and he could say all the things he had hardly dared to admit, even to himself, and they would all dissolve as if he had never said them once they got out of the car.

Kit felt her heart twist with anger and pity. 'How can you be so calm about it?'

'I really don't think there's much to worry about. But I like to be prepared. When I'm not, something irritating tends to happen.'

He was so *unmoved*. 'I see,' said Kit. She was depressed by this further evidence of how different they were.

'For example, that night we went up to look at the waterfall—strictly speaking, I should have checked in with my minder before I took you up there.'

Kit sat in silence for a bit.

Then she said slowly, 'You blame yourself for that, don't you? That General Whatsisname tracking us down? You think you shouldn't have let it happen.'

'I shouldn't have put someone else in danger,' said Philip with finality.

Last time he had said that it was unforgivable that he had put *her* in danger, thought Kit with a little catch of the heart. Now it was just someone else. If only he saw *me*, she thought.

She said slowly, 'Do you have to check with some sort of security person every time you do anything on your own?'

'When we're on a mission we're supposed to, yes.'

'And when you're not?'

'You leave your itinerary. Just in case.'

She pulled a face. 'Sounds like a real pain.'

'It certainly limits the ability to involve anyone else very deeply in one's life,' said Philip carefully.

She looked at him under her lashes. He was studying the sun-dappled road but his profile was as harsh as if it had been chipped out of marble.

She said recklessly, 'Is that a coded message?'

His mouth thinned but he did not answer.

'Solution: don't get serious about me because I can't commit. Is that it?'

He said evenly, 'I don't want there to be any misunderstandings.'

'Very good of you,' said Kit. She was simmering with anger. 'Well, neither do I. I'm here as your gopher. Neither more nor less than that.'

He said distantly, 'Of course.'

She swung round in her seat to look at that chiselled profile.

'And if you want any more,' she said with determination, 'I'm telling you now, you're going to have to work really, really hard to persuade me.'

The chiselled profile dissolved into pure appreciation.

'You're on,' said Philip.

CHAPTER EIGHT

HE BEGAN his campaign, if campaign it was, as soon as they came in sight of Ashbarrow. Kit saw the signposts. The lanes got narrower. And then they were on the crown of a hill, looking down into a secret valley.

'Oh—' she said on a long note of discovery.

The house was part castle, part Elizabethan manor house, set in the middle of a lake. In the spring sun it glowed as if there was light inside it. The castle part was stone, massive and butter coloured. The manor was darker brick, rosy in the sun, interspersed with dark beams and leaded windows.

The lake shifted gently. There were willows along its banks. Their yellow-green branches wafted like fairies' hair in the light breeze. Ducks paddled and dived busily. Irises waved among the rushes at the margin. The greensward outside the castle gates was studded with daisies like jewels.

It was perfect. Kit stared and stared.

'How could you ever bear to leave this place?' she said on a long breath.

Philip looked down at her, surprised. The green eyes were as bright as the young leaves. They sparkled with tears.

'Hey,' he said softly, 'it's only bricks and mortar.'

'But it's your home.' She sounded choked.

He could not resist it. He put his arm around her.

Kit was shaken. 'You gave up so much, didn't you? Not just all the travelling and the lack of friends. You went into exile from paradise.'

Soft blonde strands blew against his lips. Philip breathed in cleanliness and spring flowers and the soft warmth of a woman.

'Perhaps I did,' he said, shaken in his turn.

They did not speak as he drove them slowly down to the house.

As soon as they arrived Kit jumped out of the car. She still felt unaccountably tearful. She had to be careful, or this highly charged atmosphere would get to her, she thought. So she did not wait for him to open the car door for her. And she stood well out of range of that sustaining arm.

'Right,' she said with creditable briskness. 'What do you want me to do?'

He appeared amused. 'Settle in?' he suggested mildly.

'I'm here to work,' Kit scolded. 'Don't forget that. Where shall I start? Make up beds? Prepare a meal?'

He looked even more amused. 'I think the housekeeper will have done that.'

She sucked her teeth, trying not to wince. Of course there was a housekeeper. There was bound to be a housekeeper.

It was going to be like France all over again. She had rattled round in her brother-in-law's family château, making social gaffe after social gaffe. This was where it started all over again.

'I give you fair warning,' she said in a matter-of-fact tone, 'I'm not grand enough for this place.'

Philip was leafing through some letters on the hall table but he looked up at that.

'What on earth do you mean?'

The table was a great slab of oak. Thirty monks could dine off it if they had to, thought Kit, and probably had in their day. It was polished until you could see your face in it. Philip paid it no more attention than if it had been a supermarket check-out counter.

'Look at you,' she said, waving a hand at the ripped envelope. 'You're making a garbage pile out of an antique.'

He was laughing at her. 'So? It will all get tidied up in time.'

'Don't tell me. By the housekeeper,' she said gloomily. 'What am I doing here?'

'Giving me advice,' he retorted. Adding mischievously, 'And making me work really, really hard to persuade you to like me.'

Kit flushed, suddenly uncertain. He was laughing. But his eyes...his eyes were not laughing. His eyes were very, very serious. She felt heat flood through her.

And then a heavy door from another part of the house opened and the housekeeper arrived.

The housekeeper was a shock. This was not the tight-lipped gorgon with standards that Kit had expected. She was not much older than Kit and she was wearing jeans and an orange sweatshirt. And she did not curtsey to Philip either.

'Oh, hi, Phil. Thought I heard your car,' she said casually.

'Hello, Sandy. This is Kit.'

The housekeeper stripped off a bright yellow rubber glove and shook hands enthusiastically. 'Great to see you. I really hope you're comfortable. I've made up the Queen's Room, like you said, Phil. But that old bed doesn't have any springs, you know. It's beautiful but you might have trouble sleeping,' she told Kit frankly.

There were so many answers to that—and all of them equivocal in one way or another—that Kit was silenced.

She avoided Philip's eyes as he said blandly, 'We'll see. Anyway, I can deal with that when the time comes.'

He took Kit's hand unselfconsciously. 'Let me show you to your room.'

She went with him, trying hard to look as if she held hands with tall, dark, handsome aristocrats every day of the week. And hoping that her ears weren't as pink as she thought they were.

But when they got to the Queen's Room she forgot embarrassment in simple wonder.

The room was dominated by a massive tester bed. The canopy was hung with curtains of velvet as green as all the spring loveliness outside. And the coverlet was like liquid sunshine.

'Cloth of gold,' said Philip, seeing the direction of her gaze. 'Looks wonderful. Scratches like the devil.'

Kit put a hand on it very gently, as if she thought it was a mirage that might dissolve.

He said lightly, 'You know, from the first day I saw you I thought that you were meant for this room.'

She looked up at him, startled.

'But now,' said Philip softly, 'I see I was wrong.'

Kit was shocked at how that stabbed. She turned away.

'Of course,' she said in a brittle voice. 'I told you I wasn't grand enough for this place.'

'I wanted to see you lying on that coverlet,' he went on as if she had not spoken. 'But, of course, it's out of the question. You'd have to keep your clothes on or get scratched to pieces.'

'Oh!' said Kit in quite a different voice.

'And if I persuade you I'm nice enough to take you to bed,' said Philip, his voice suddenly ragged, 'you sure as hell aren't doing it with your clothes on.'

Kit felt her eyes widening and widening. Not just her ears, her whole body must be pink, she thought. Her heart sang. But her brain said, Hang on. This is where you go marching up the path into uncharted territory. You made a complete pig's ear of it last time. It's only fair to tell him what he's tangling with.

'Say something,' he teased, his eyes on her mouth. 'If it's only ''Dream on!'''

Kit gulped. 'I wasn't going to say that.' Her voice sounded strange. 'But—'

Philip cocked a wicked eyebrow. 'I haven't worked really, really hard enough yet?'

'No, you haven't,' said Kit with some return of spirit. 'But I wasn't going to say that either. It's—'

'You have a prejudice against housekeepers. Don't worry. Sandy goes home at five.'

'Stop it,' said Kit fiercely. 'I've told you before about finishing my sentences.'

He flung his hands up in a gesture of surrender.

She pulled herself together, marshalling her thoughts with difficulty.

'Look,' she said at last. 'You don't know as much about me as you think you do. There's something I ought to tell you.'

'You're married with four children?' Philip's eyes were alight with laughter.

It was difficult to resist the temptation to laugh back. 'No, of course not.'

'Anything else I can handle,' he said superbly.

Kit smiled. 'Maybe you can. Let me tell you first.'

'Tell me anything you want.' He held out his hand. 'Let me take you round my castle and you can tell me the terrible truth.'

It was amazingly difficult. Kit had not talked about it for so long, she had forgotten how, she thought. And of course for some of it she had no words, because she had never talked at all.

In the end she stopped dead in front of a picture of a lot of mediaeval people scampering about a forest and stared at it unseeingly.

'The Utrillo,' said Philip, pleased. 'You like that?'

Kit nodded, not attending.

'I know what you think of me,' she told the unicorn, dancing through the midnight trees. Somehow it was easier not to look at him while she told him her secrets. 'You think I'm young and innocent and sensitive.'

'And sexy as hell. Don't forget that.'

'Thank you.' She couldn't look at him even more after that. 'But I'm not innocent. Not in the way you think I am.'

'Are you trying to tell me you slept with the boy who was not in love with you?' he said gently.

Kit jumped. She had forgotten she had told him that.

'You're an adult,' he said, shrugging. 'Sexual experience goes with the territory.' His eyes glinted down at her. 'It's probably one of the few things we have in common.'

She smiled but she shook her head. 'I'm not making a sexual confession. It's about me, the mess I made—I— Oh, dammit.' She swung round on him as if he was an enemy. 'I was anorexic,' she blurted. 'Before I was a teenager. Oh, I got better. Lisa helped. Then Johnny didn't want me and—well, something else happened too. And I just fell apart. The whole thing started again. Hating myself. Not looking in mirrors. Not wanting anyone to look at me.'

'Oh, Kit! My poor love.'

Philip was no longer even thinking of laughing. He wanted to put his arms round her and suddenly did not dare.

She looked away. 'Lisa helped me get through that too. She found me a therapist. He said to look at what I want, not what other people wanted for me.'

'You're over it, then?'

Kit drew a shaky breath. 'Who knows? There are as many different patterns as there are cures. The last man I went to said that he thought in my case it was probably an idea that had been implanted early, because I started so young. If I could dig that out I might dare to say I'm cured. But I don't know if he's right or how the idea got fixed. We even did some hypnotherapy and couldn't find it. So maybe he's wrong.'

Philip looked at her gravely. 'And you think that if you let me make love to you you're risking it starting up again?'

Kit shook her head decisively. 'No. Not that. I know the signs. I can handle stress now.'

'Then what?' said Philip. 'Because you're afraid of something, aren't you?'

Kit looked at the unicorn in the painting, so gallant. So heedlessly hopeful. The unicorn did not know that there was anything to fear from those men creeping through the woods after it. But she did. She did.

'People hurt you,' she said. 'They're having a good time, so they don't notice. But you notice. And you don't get over it.'

He could not bear it. He put his arm round her and pulled her against his side.

'Are you telling me you haven't got over Johnny?'

She shook her head again, violently.

'What, then? What haven't you got over, my love?'

She did not remember that she had told him never to mention the word love to her again. She said baldly, 'I should have had a baby.'

There was absolute silence. Then Philip said in his most gentle, controlled voice, 'You're right. This needs talking about. Come with me.'

They went to a small sitting room. There was a great copper jug of cherry blossom in the grate and the leaded windows stood open to the spring sun.

Philip sat her in a tapestry chair and pulled up a battered footstool to sit by her feet. He took her hands and held on to them.

'Tell me.'

She swallowed. 'I had a crush on him. He wasn't really interested. But it was convenient to have someone to go to parties with on campus, I suppose. We only made love a couple of times.' She looked up. 'It was as much my responsibility as his. I made all the running,' she said, anxious to be clear. 'I don't want you to think I was some sort of victim.'

Philip pushed a soft strand of hair behind her ear as if he could not help himself.

'Something else we have in common, then. I always want to be fair, too.'

She gave him a sweet, surprised smile. 'I think you could just be my hero.'

She did not notice the effect that had on him. Philip saw it ruefully. He kept hold of her hands.

She said with difficulty, 'I thought I was pregnant. Well, I was nearly certain. I told Johnny. He went ballistic.'

She could still see his face. White and furious. She shivered slightly. Philip's hold tightened.

'Probably he was frightened as much as angry,' he said in his calmest voice. Though he could have killed the young idiot who was making his darling shake with remembered grief.

She nodded. 'Maybe. At the time all I knew was that he hated me. He shook me.'

Philip's hands clenched on hers like a vice. He looked dangerous suddenly. Hundreds of combatants around the world would not have recognised their rock-like peace negotiator in this narrow-eyed man. Catching sight of his face in the mirror beyond her shoulder, Philip did not recognise himself either.

Kit eased her pinched fingers. Philip looked down, remorseful. She shook her head. 'I'm all right. Though for a long time I didn't want anyone to touch me. I'm probably over that now. After Coral Cove.'

It was like being given everything he had ever dreamed of. And she did not even realise what she had said. She was sitting there. Frowning as she strove to tell him her horrible secrets, when she had already told him the only thing in the world that mattered.

I am going to make her so happy, Philip promised himself. *I am going to make her the happiest woman in the world.*

'Only—I ran away. It was a filthy night and I just ran. Walked and walked. Got soaked and still carried on walking. And then I went to get the bus home. The steps were wet. I fell down them. A long concrete flight.'

'You lost the baby,' said Philip quietly, understanding at last.

Kit gave a laugh that broke in the middle. 'Not even that. They said in the hospital that it was a false alarm. That I had never been pregnant at all. And I thought that they were lying.'

'Why would they do that?'

'Spare my feelings. People always want to spare my feelings. As if I'm too feeble to cope with life as it is. Too feeble to protect my own baby.' She sounded as if she hated herself.

Philip said sharply, 'You're not feeble and doctors don't lie to spare people's feelings. They're too worried about lawsuits.'

Kit raised her head.

He said, 'If you want a reason to beat yourself up, find a better one than that.'

She searched his face and saw for the first time the narrow-eyed temper.

She echoed wonderingly, 'Beat myself up?'

'What I can't understand,' said Philip, very precise in his fury, 'is that people have let you hang on to this nonsense all these years. Even if you managed to sell it to your family, surely serious health professionals should have told you to get a grip? You did say you had a therapist?'

'Yes,' said Kit, dazed. Suddenly she wanted to laugh, to run like the unicorn, tossing her head in the air and dancing with delight. 'Yes, I did. Only I never told him about the baby. I never told anyone before today.'

'Then let this be the end of it,' said Philip soberly.

'Oh, yes. *Yes.*'

She leaned forward and rested her head against his. She could feel his strength flowing into her. He was a rock.

He said into her hair. 'I mean it, Kit. I can fight rivals. I can fight the world if I have to. I can't fight what's going on in your own head.'

She looked up then and took his head between her hands. She kissed him full on the mouth.

'You don't have to. I'm all right now. I will always be all right. With you.'

He took her round his kingdom. He took her to all his favourite places and offered them to her, as if he was a knight returning from a quest with all that was precious in the world.

He took her along the portrait gallery, going from ruffled ancestor to ancestor.

'My family are a cold and unforgiving lot. They don't trust easily. If they do trust and it is betrayed they pursue the betrayer forever.'

Kit looked at a wall full of uncompromising jaws and steady eyes, so like Philip's own, and believed him.

They went to the old castle guardroom with its arrow-slit windows and flagstone floor.

'I used to play Ivanhoe here,' said Philip with a reminiscent smile. 'The stone makes a wonderful clang if you hit it with your sword.'

'They gave you a sword to play with?' said Kit, appalled at the recklessness of the upper classes in the matter of child rearing.

He laughed aloud at that. 'The drawing-room poker. I'll show you.'

They went through the stables.

'My grandfather said I could only have a pony as long as I groomed him myself.' Philip ran his hand up a beam, looking at the empty stalls. 'When I went away to school he was sold.'

'He sounds tough.'

'He was. Fair, though. Just not very warm.'

Kit walked into the curve of his arm, laying her cheek on his shoulder as if she would compensate for all the warmth he had missed without knowing it. She rubbed her cheek against his cashmere sweater.

'Who did you play with?'

He looked down at her, amused. 'Now this is where your prejudice against the upper classes is going to come into its own. My grandfather had my nanny import two boys from the village for the purpose. On Saturday afternoons. It meant they missed football. They hated it.'

'Oppressor of the poor,' said Kit, twinkling.

'Completely. We became good friends, though. One of them is now my land agent. One of them is the local postman. Married to Sandy, whom you've met.'

She made a face at him. 'Feudal lord!'

They linked hands and wandered out into the sunshine.

'Did you ever play when it hadn't been planned in advance?' Kit asked curiously.

His eyes danced. 'Not until now.'

She did not laugh back at him. 'Then we'd better make it worth waiting for,' she said, looking at him steadily.

And slid her hands under the sweater.

His eyes flared.

'Are you sure?' he said in a low voice.

She nodded.

That was when he took her to his own room.

This was different. It did not have the golds and velvets and elaborate carving of the Queen's Room. It did not have priceless paintings or great urns of ceremonial flowers. It was simple and homely and *his*.

The moment Kit walked into it, she knew she was in the right place. It was almost as if she had been here before. She recognised a tie on the chair. He had worn it at that fateful reception at Coral Cove. The room spoke of him. It felt like home.

'Looks as if Sandy has already been in,' he said. 'She always dives on my suitcases, looking for washing. But just in case—'

He turned the massive iron key in the lock and came to her.

Now that she was here, she was nervous again. Not scared. She could never be scared of Philip.

But aware that she had never done this before. Never gone to bed in the middle of the day and stone-cold sober with a man who looked as if she was about to give him the world.

She said worriedly, 'When I said I wasn't an innocent I didn't mean that Mata Hari could take my correspondence course. I mean, I'm not all *that* experienced.'

'I am,' said Philip, amused.

Kit ignored this frivolity. 'It isn't that I haven't done this before. Well, not exactly this, maybe. But I haven't done it for a long time. And never, well, never—'

'Never with me,' said Philip calmly. 'Another thing we have in common.'

'Yes, all right. I suppose so. But it feels—'

He slid hands that were warm and sure under her T-shirt.

'Yes?' he prompted mischievously. 'How does it feel?'

Kit gave a deep, voluptuous shiver.

'Strange,' she said, suddenly hoarse.

'And that?'

She swallowed. 'I could get used to it.'

He shook his head. 'Now there's a challenge.'

Kit looked deep into his eyes. She had never done anything like this, she realised. Never looked into a man's eyes and desired and teased and loved.

Loved?

She felt it slide through her, like water flooding a lock. It filled her, made her tingle, made her *yearn*.

She stood up very straight and pulled the T-shirt over her head. From the look on his face, she saw that Philip knew how big a step it was for her.

She melted into his arms. She kept her eyes tight shut, hearing his hurried breathing, her own galloping pulse, the creaks of the old house, the call of the birds outside the window...

Philip said her name in a voice that did not sound like his at all.

She began to tug at his clothes with fingers that were clumsy and unfamiliar. He stilled them.

'Slowly.' It was a ragged whisper.

'I want,' said Kit, panting. 'I want—'

But she couldn't say what she wanted. Any more than she could open her eyes.

He picked her up. Her heart lurched and her eyes flew open.

'Better,' said Philip, still ragged.

He carried her to the bed and pushed the sober navy duvet aside. With one knee on the bed, he lowered her as gently as if she was a precious device and withdrew his arms. He touched her face, gently, possessively, as if he could not believe she was here in his bed.

Kit caught his hand and carried it to her lips.

She saw his reaction that time all right. But still he held off from her.

'Don't close your eyes, Kit,' he said as if it was dragged out of him. 'Don't shut me out.'

It was not an order. This was no longer the all-powerful negotiator, calm and godlike, she saw, wondering. This was a man who did not know his way through the maze any better than she did.

For a moment she thought she would drown in panic. And then she did the bravest thing she had ever done in her life.

She mastered the stupid embarrassment that was not doing either of them any good.

And sat up.

And wriggled out of the rest of her clothes.

And sank back naked among his pillows and held her arms out.

'Look at me,' said Kit, with a catch in her voice. 'Love me.'

CHAPTER NINE

HE MADE love to her with his whole heart. Kit was quite certain of that. No matter how limited and long ago her sexual experience had been, there was no mistaking that. She had never felt so cared for in her life.

He was right, he did know more than she did. A lot more about the rhythms of her body as well as his. A lot more about how to sensitise her flesh and then take her to the pinnacle of sensation and beyond.

'Where have you been all my life?' she gasped at one point, when she could speak again.

He laughed in his throat. 'Just waiting for someone who would appreciate my expertise properly to come along.'

And he bent again to his self-appointed task of driving her wild.

But it was not the expertise that captured her heart. Nor the laughter, though she had never thought people could laugh as they made love and it enchanted her. It made her feel as if they were equals as well as lovers and could laugh at the world together. It was the way he treasured her. The way he looked at her. The way he never stopped looking, even when his own body convulsed in shattering climax. The way he seemed to look straight into her heart.

'And I thought I didn't like people looking at me,' said Kit, disconcerted, when at last they could talk again. She sounded bemused and not a little shocked.

Philip held her against his shoulder and looped some blonde hair around her ear.

'Good.'

'What?' She was put out.

'Stick with that thought. I'm not people. I'm your lover.' He kissed her temple softly. 'No one else needs to look at you. Keep all the others off with boat hooks and grappling irons.'

Kit's eyes drifted closed at the caress. She gave a dreamy chuckle. 'I take it you played pirates as well as Ivanhoe?'

'With a lake on the premises? What do you think?'

It was wonderful lying together as the sun set behind the hill beyond his window. It was wonderful to talk nonsense and know that he understood, as she understood him. Every shared joke bonded them closer. Every possessive touch welded them further into a couple.

'I never knew it could be like this,' she said softly.

He stroked her arm with the tips of his fingers. 'Nor me.'

She nestled against his chest. He was hairier than you would expect from his fine-boned face and smooth, well-kept hands. It made Kit feel as if she knew a secret about him—that under the conservative suits and restrained manner he was flesh and blood. And vulnerable to passion, after all.

Oh, boy, was he vulnerable to passion, she thought, stretching luxuriously along the length of his tall body.

He caught her hand and held it to his chest. 'Comfortable?'

She flexed her fingers under his, feeling the structure of bone and muscle, the warmth of skin. She felt as if she had never been so close to another human being. She thought in wonder, *Who would have believed I could ever do this? Feel this?*

'Mmm. Every bit of me is comfortable,' she assured him, beginning to slur. 'Never been so comfortable.'

'Good.'

Even with her head on his shoulder, she could feel him smile.

Feel him smile? Boy, have I got it bad, thought Kit drowsily.

She murmured, 'Philip?'

'Yes?'

'Love you,' she said on a massive yawn.

And fell asleep.

So she did not know that Philip stayed awake, staring at the darkening landscape. He held her strongly, protectively. But the laughter died away. Along with the warmth.

Philip Hardesty, cradling his sleeping unicorn girl, viewed a suddenly uncertain future. A future which had just slipped out of his control. If he let it.

'Live for today,' she had said. But how could he? How *could* he?

He had watched so many colleagues' marriages founder on the absences, the sheer preoccupied business of being a peace negotiator. Families receded into the background for weeks, months at a time. And the danger! He knew how sensitive she was. He had seen it. How would she cope with him not only being away but being a target as well?

It would not be fair to ask her. It would not be fair to any woman.

But I don't want to be fair.

Philip thought about it for a long time as, beyond the window, the moon began to rise. His face grew stern. Slowly, imperceptibly, his shoulders tensed, as if he was taking up an invisible burden again.

He curved his hand lightly along Kit's bare arm. The unseen caress spoke of longing and an almost unbearable tenderness. But it was no longer possessive.

And Kit slept on, unaware.

For Kit the days that followed were magical. As the blossom opened and the sun intensified it seemed she was opening to new life as well. It went to her head like wine. She did not notice anything except how happy she was.

She walked with Philip in the gardens, scrambled through Ashbarrow Woods with him, and sat in the fire-lit drawing room, holding hands with him. When they had been apart for an hour she went into the library where he was working on his computer. And he closed the thing down at once and held out his hand to her, as if she was his guardian angel.

And all the time she talked. How she talked!

She told him about how she had always needed to move from job to job, so no one could pin her down. She wandered through Ashbarrow's impressive china cupboards in his bathrobe, fingering gold-edged antique crockery, and told him without bitterness about her mother's economies when they were children. She drifted round the panelled music room with him and admitted her failure with the piano concerto in spite of her valiant self-improvement programme.

'And opera is turning out to be a real struggle too,' she said gloomily.

When Philip stopped laughing he played her a CD of such unearthly beauty that Kit was moved almost to tears.

'Opera?' she said as the pure notes died away at last.

Philip's face was inscrutable for a moment. 'Opera. Handel, actually. Not fashionable but I like him.'

'What does it mean?' said Kit softly.

He hesitated for a moment. 'Something like, "Where are you, my darling? You are the only who stands between me and despair."'

There was a little silence. Kit sat very still. She found she was holding her breath. She did not know why.

Then he seemed to come out of a reverie and said in quite a different tone, '*Rodelinda*. Seriously melodramatic stuff. But the music is exquisite.'

And the moment, whatever it was, passed. She even forgot about it.

Until the next morning. Kit was sitting with him in the library, where a sixteenth-century Hardesty ancestor had composed a blueprint for a just society. Later an eighteenth-century one had written poems at the very desk that stood in the corner. Kit found she had even read one.

'He was the black sheep,' said Philip lazily, drawing her hair through his fingers and holding it up to the morning sun.

They were sitting in the window seat together, drinking instant coffee from kitchen mugs. They had twenty minutes left with the house to themselves before Sandy arrived. They were making the most of it. Kit was wearing his shirt and nothing else. She felt wonderful.

'A black sheep? Why?'

He pulled a face. 'Poetry? Pure self-indulgence! Hardestys were soldiers. They were supposed to do their duty, not mess about writing wimpy poetry.'

Kit pulled his arm a little tighter round her waist. 'You mean like you do,' she said soberly.

There was the faintest pause before he said, 'I suppose so.'

There it was again. That faint note of withdrawal. She frowned, not knowing what to do.

This is where it would help to be an experienced woman. Instead of someone who has only just given up avoiding mirrors.

The thought reminded her of something.

She said, 'I ought to go and see my godmother. She can't be that far away from here.'

His arm tensed at once. It was almost as if he was flinching away from the idea. Kit cork-screwed round to look up at him.

'Philip?'

He was smiling. Not the warm, intimate smile that she had thought she would always get from him now, but a tighter, cooler expression alto-gether. Kit was chilled.

'Philip?' she said again. 'What's wrong?'

'Nothing,' he said at once. 'You want to go and see your godmother. Of course.'

He's jealous, she thought on a little rush of relief. She put up a hand to touch his face.

'Not on my own, stupid. I want us to go to-gether.'

He hesitated infinitesimally.

'Don't you want to?' she said, suddenly alarmed and not sure why.

To her inexpressible relief, his smile got real again. He bent forward and kissed her lightly.

'I'd really like to,' she said, still not quite re-assured.

'Then we will.'

But the lovely, careless closeness was gone.

It happened again and again, over the day.

First, Kit saw the morning sun refracting into a thousand colours out of a dewdrop on a leaf just outside the kitchen window. She turned to Philip to share it. He was supposed to be slicing bread for their breakfast toast, but he had stopped mid action. He was staring into space with an expression so grim that it struck her to the heart. She closed the window quietly. He did not notice.

It was the same when she asked about one of the modern portraits. It was in the big dining room, which they had not used. It showed a queenly woman in three-quarter profile. Her dark hair was swept up into a coronet and she wore a tiara and magnificent jewels. But what caught Kit's attention was her expression. She looked as if she was wound so tight, she was about to break.

'That one?' said Philip neutrally. 'That's a Bosco. Before he got into his modernist phase, of course. Still very collectible, I'm told.'

Kit shook her head. 'You're labelling again,' she teased. 'I don't care about the painter. Who is *she*?'

'My mother,' said Philip, even more neutral.

Kit stared up at the painting. 'She doesn't look happy,' she said slowly.

He shrugged. 'Shows what a good painter Bosco was. She wasn't.'

'But she was so beautiful,' said Kit slowly. 'And that necklace! What made her so unhappy that she couldn't enjoy it?'

He hesitated. 'My father's job.'

Kit frowned. 'Diplomat?'

'And soldier. You never really leave the army behind, even when you're military attaché at an embassy. She grew to hate it.'

'Why?'

He went closer to the picture and looked up at it, frowning slightly.

'I suppose it was more dangerous than she expected,' he said slowly. 'They met in Cambridge. No assassination attempts there. By the time this was painted they had been in Africa and the Gulf and he had survived two car bombs and kidnap at knifepoint. She couldn't cope.'

Kit did not quite know why, but she sensed a deep despair in him. She stepped closer and nudged him with her shoulder.

'Well, she got to wear some pretty good dresses,' she said cheerfully. 'She looks as if she's going to be crowned.'

Philip gave a crack of laughter. 'My father's regimental ball, actually. There's a companion portrait of him in the study. All scarlet coat and medals.'

Kit looked up at him. 'That's your father? I thought he was another Victorian.'

'Well spotted,' said Philip, darkly amused. 'Neither he nor my grandfather had much truck with the twentieth century. Men did their duty. Women were grateful. Children were seen and not heard.' His amusement died. 'It broke my mother. Party dresses and diamonds didn't begin to compensate.'

Kit shrank closer. 'No, they wouldn't,' she said compassionately. 'But she loved him?'

His arm fell, leaving her bereft. Their shoulders no longer touched.

'Oh, yes, she loved him,' he said heavily.

'Then that would have been enough.'

He looked down at her unsmilingly. 'Didn't seem to be. But then, what do I know?'

And the grim expression was back.

Kit shivered. She did not know why.

And then he was charm itself to Aunt Flora. And remote as the Atlas Mountains. Kit could see her godmother getting more and more uneasy as they sat in her tiny, crowded sitting room. It made Kit uneasy herself. She tried to get reassurance from Philip but he seemed to avoid her eyes.

What's wrong? Has he decided I'm not good enough for Ashbarrow now he's seen Flora's cottage?

It was an unsettling thought. She didn't believe it but— Why else was there that distance between them? Why wouldn't he look at her?

In the end she couldn't bear the tension any longer. She said, 'I think I'll just ring Tatiana.

Just to make sure she isn't turning the hose on my visiting cat.'

Perhaps Philip would be himself again if he didn't feel she was watching him perform for her godmother, she thought. She escaped to the hall, where Flora's old-fashioned telephone was tucked into an alcove.

Left alone, Flora let Philip make fluent small talk for a few minutes. Then she looked up and said abruptly, 'Kit has told you about her problems, hasn't she?' She made no apology for interrupting him.

Philip stiffened. 'I know about the anorexia, if that's what you mean.'

Flora nodded, sad and satisfied at the same time. 'I thought she would. She's a chivalrous girl. Tell you it's over, did she?'

Philip said gently, 'You can't expect that I would repeat our private conversations to you.'

Flora stared at him for silent moments from under her fierce eyebrows. In the end she seemed to be satisfied with what she saw. She gave a jerky nod.

'Well, maybe she is. I don't know. I do know that she's too tender-hearted for her own good.'

Philip watched her calmly. He did not answer.

Flora did not seem to expect him to. She said reminiscently, 'She was always like that, even as a child. She used to stay here, you know. Well,

I was glad to give her mother a break. I felt sorry for Joanne. An extra mouth to feed only two weeks after her husband walked out!'

Philip's brows knit hard at that.

Flora did not notice. 'Lisa and Kit used to come and stay together. But it was always Kit who used to bring wounded things home. Birds with broken wings. A badger hit by a car. We were always trailing off to the vet. Cost me a fortune. But, to be fair, she always nursed them herself when we got them back here.' She looked at him very straightly. 'She's always wanted to heal things, my Kit.'

He drew a sharp breath.

But whatever he was going to say was overtaken by Kit exploding back into the room. She looked distraught. Philip leaped to his feet, the remote look utterly banished.

'What is it?' he said, taking her hands.

She returned the grip instinctively.

'It's Lisa. Tatiana says— Oh, I can't believe it.'

'Then tell us and see if we believe it,' said Flora practically.

'Tatiana says that Lisa is leaving Nikolai.' Kit's voice shook.

Philip frowned.

Kit's eyes were full of tears. 'I'm really afraid it's all my fault.'

'Oh, please!' Flora was crisp.

But Philip said in his most neutral, reasonable voice, 'Have you any evidence for that?'

Kit gave him an edgy look and pulled her hands away. 'Don't do the professional-negotiator bit on me,' she said with sudden sharpness. 'She *told* me. They were having a difficult time in Coral Cove. But they made up. And then they had a row about me just before she came back to London. About *me*. I must go to her.'

'People don't end a marriage over their sister-in-law,' Flora announced.

'I'm bound to agree,' said Philip, still maddeningly logical. 'Did you speak to Lisa yourself?'

'No—'

'Then don't you think you'd better? Maybe this Tatiana has got the wrong end of the stick.'

'More than likely,' muttered Flora.

'I haven't got Lisa's number,' said Kit. She looked sick. 'She's in Zurich. I don't know her number at work.'

'I do,' said Philip calmly.

They both stared at him.

He said to Flora, 'When I was looking for Kit I tried everyone I could think of. I never managed to catch up with her. But I certainly have the number of the Zurich office in my laptop at home.'

'Then let's go,' said Kit.

She kissed her godmother distractedly and nearly forgot her coat. She sat on the edge of her seat all the way back in the car.

Philip said levelly, 'I'm with your godmother on this. Don't highjack Lisa's problems.'

Kit bounced round on the seat. *What?*

'It's nothing to do with you—'

She said between her teeth, 'My sister has never let me down. I'm not going to walk away from her now.'

Philip's mouth tightened. He said nothing for a moment. Then—in his coolest, calmest voice—'Let's look at this logically—'

Kit exploded.

She told him her sister's disaster was not a matter of logic. She told him that he knew nothing about family. Nothing about feelings. Nothing about sticking to the people who loved you.

'You sit on the fence for a living,' she ended up, panting a little.

Philip was white round the mouth.

But he was still very much master of himself. 'I think we'd better put off further discussion until we're home.'

'Home!' raged Kit. 'Ancient monument, more like. You don't know one thing about—'

'Enough!' said Philip with such icy force that she was silenced.

But she did not forgive him. As soon as they pulled up outside the house she leaped out and ran for the door, without waiting for him. He followed and found her in the library, turning his computer on with frenzied jabbing movements.

'Find me Lisa's phone number,' she commanded.

Quietly he showed her his address list. There were hundreds of entries, Kit saw as he scrolled down. The office of President This. The international secretariat of that. It told its own story, all too clearly.

It wasn't Ashbarrow she wasn't good enough for. It was Philip Hardesty, mentor of presidents. It chilled her to the bone. If she hadn't been so agitated about Lisa she would have wept.

She gave an unsmiling nod to acknowledge his help and picked up the phone.

'I'll get you a coffee,' he said, quite as if he did not have the world to run.

Kit swallowed wretchedly. But she did not say anything.

When he came back with two mugs she was sitting at Sir Oliver Hardesty's fine walnut kneehole desk, with the telephone restored to its cradle. She looked stunned.

He put the coffee down on a mat in front of her. She shook her head as if to clear it.

'She's coming home.'

'So you spoke to her?'

'Yes.' Kit swallowed. 'I must go back to London. Be with her.'

'Leave them to sort out their own business,' Philip advised.

She stared at him as if she did not know who he was.

He said, 'I wasn't going to tell you but—I have to go back at the end of the week. We only have three more days together.'

'Go *back*?'

'I got an email this morning. I'm needed in Pelanang. I leave on Friday.'

Kit was blank. 'You agreed to go back without even mentioning it to me?'

He smiled faintly. 'They're not used to my taking holiday. My office didn't think they needed to check with me first. They never have before.'

'Of course not,' said Kit in a thin little voice. 'And why should they now?'

She lifted her head and met his eyes straightly. 'Why should they?' she repeated harshly. 'What's changed, after all?'

There was an infinitesimal pause. Then he said roughly, 'I knew this would happen.'

Kit was shaking. 'Of course you did.' She was angry, she told herself. More than angry. She was *furious*. 'What else can you expect from a girl who thinks people are more important than labels?'

'Kit—'

'I expect it comes from a lack of illustrious ancestors.' It was a very good imitation of his own analytical manner. 'Yes, that would account for it. No sense of duty.'

'*Kit!*'

She looked round the beautiful room with its panelling and its leather-bound books.

Philip saw her anger, her hurt and did not know what to do. All his training was no use here. He was lost.

'What has that got to do with anything?' He sounded exasperated, which was not what he meant at all.

But she gave him no time to retrieve his error.

'You didn't want me to get the wrong idea, did you?' Kit flung at him. 'Girls from the wrong side of the tracks are only allowed in on day passes.'

'You've had a lot more than a day pass,' he protested on a reflex he immediately regretted.

She pounced. '*Had?* So I'm on my way out now, am I?'

'Of course not.' Philip strove to calm the atmosphere. 'Look at the facts for a moment. You were the one saying you had to go.'

She glared, mutinous.

He tried again. 'Be fair. I was begging you to stay, if you remember.'

Kit took a deep breath. 'For how long?'

He did not answer. But he flinched. It was all the answer she needed.

The silence stretched, horrifying them both.

She said, almost inaudibly, 'I'd like to go now, please.'

Philip was very pale. But all he said was, 'There's no need.' And then, with fatal politeness, 'You're welcome to stay at Ashbarrow as long as you like.'

Kit's eyes flashed.

He said wretchedly, 'No, I didn't meant that. Well, not the way it sounded. Kit, please—'

But she was turning away. She was icy now.

'I'm sure there must be a train. Could you order me a taxi, please? I'd like to go to the nearest station as soon as possible.'

'I'll take you.'

That got through the ice all right.

'*No!*'

But Philip was adamant. 'I brought you down here. I'll drive you back.'

She gave up.

They did not speak in the car. But he kept putting his hand up to his left eye as if he were trying to brush a cobweb or something away from it.

Eventually Kit said, 'Is your eye hurting?'

'Hurting?' He was curt. 'No.'

'Then you can't see out of it,' she deduced. 'You'd better stop the car and let me drive.'

To her astonishment, he did.

When they were on the road again he said in a low voice, 'Kit, I never meant to mislead you.'

She did not speak. She was too new a driver to concentrate on anything but the road. And anyway, what was there to say?

He went on, 'My job is—well, you've seen it.' He gave an abrupt, unamused laugh. 'I always promised my mother I wouldn't go into the army. So I end up with a job that's even worse!' He shook his head. 'I can't ask a woman to share a life like that.'

You could try.

But she didn't say it. How could she?

She was not the woman for him. She could not wear dresses that looked as if they were made for a coronation and diamonds in her hair. She could not run a house like Ashbarrow. She did not have eighteenth-century ancestors who wrote liberal poetry. Her ancestors had probably not even been able to read, thought Kit, struggling to apply common sense.

Of course he couldn't marry her. Quite apart from his ancestry, he was an important man. The world needed him, all of him.

But so do I.

She set her teeth. She could not afford to cry while she was driving.

They went the rest of the way in silence.

He roused himself to direct her once they reached the outskirts of London. His voice was quite impersonal. Neither friendly nor unfriendly.

You would have thought they had never made love in the evening sun nor awoken to look at the rising moon. You would have thought they had never touched at all. The distance between them was total.

Kit felt her heart would break and nearly ran a red light.

'Careful,' said Philip unemotionally.

She drew a shaky breath and concentrated harder. She got them back to the Notting Hill house in one piece and switched off the engine. The keys rattled as she did so. That was when Kit realised she was trembling, slightly but convulsively, right the way down to her toes. It was as if she had had a bad shock. Which she had in a way, she supposed.

She slid out of the car, not looking at him.

Philip got out and came round to her. He took her bag out of the back of the car but he did not give it to her. He stood holding it, looking down at her. His face was unreadable.

He said, 'You could come on to the hotel with me.'

Kit shook her head. 'No, I couldn't,' she said sadly.

'I don't see what you think you're going to do for your sister.'

'Be with her. Hold her hand. Listen. Make her coffee and abuse men.' It was a valiant attempt at a joke. But not brilliant in the circumstances.

He stiffened.

'Sorry,' she said.

She held out her hand for the bag. He did not give it to her.

'Stay with me.' It was harsh, sudden, as if it was wrenched out of him without his own volition.

This was awful. Kit looked at him through a mist of gathering tears.

'I *can't*.'

His face wasn't unreadable any more. He looked tortured.

'I never meant to hurt you. I didn't think—'

'It's all right,' she said gently. 'You never promised me anything. You never even said you loved me.'

He was very pale. 'I don't know what the word means. I told you. I—just don't understand love. I never have.'

Kit stared at him. Her eyes went darker and darker until there was almost no green left in them at all, Philip saw. Her trembling got worse. She was as pale as he.

'Yes, you do,' she said almost inaudibly. 'Only you're afraid of it. You think it will make you weak.'

He said nothing.

She seized the bag clumsily.

'I can't bear this.' Her voice was ragged. 'I've got to go. Goodbye.'

Philip did not move or speak. He looked as if he was in shock.

Kit wrenched the bag away from him and ran up the front steps as if the hounds of hell were after her.

And out of his life, she thought. *And out of his life.*

CHAPTER TEN

TATIANA welcomed her with open arms. All disagreements forgotten, she even let the neighbouring cat dance in from the garden and take up residence on Kit's knee. Tatiana was worried. So worried that she did not notice Kit's pallor or that she answered her questions mechanically.

'Lisa sounds terrible. I can't think what's happened.'

But Kit could. Kit knew exactly what was going on. Lisa had told her on the phone. It was what had brought her bundling back for London, even before Philip had faced her with the terrible truth about their relationship. Or rather their lack of a relationship.

'It's all right,' said Kit steadily. 'I'll look after her.'

It was just as well she was prepared. Arriving from Switzerland, Lisa did not go to the Holland Park house that Nikolai had bought after their marriage. She came straight to the flat.

Kit ran up the stairs as soon as she heard the taxi draw up in the street outside. She flung open the door and tumbled down the front steps to enfold her sister in her arms.

'Oh, *Kit*!'

And Lisa, who had fought off school bullies, stiffened her mother's backbone when Joanne said she couldn't go on and found ways to pay bills that no one else could have dreamed of— Lisa, the rock—fumbled off her dark glasses and wept on her sister's shoulder.

'It's all right,' said Kit, gentle but still mechanical. 'I promise you. It will be all right. Come in and tell me everything.'

She picked up Lisa's overnight case and urged her indoors.

Lisa sank onto the sofa. She looked ill. More than that, thought Kit, who knew a bit about tears, she looked as if she had been crying for days.

She made her the promised coffee, then sat down beside her.

'Tell me,' she said gently. 'You're pregnant and Nikolai doesn't want the baby. Why?'

Lisa shook her head. She seemed drained. 'I suppose it all started last year. I lost a baby in the autumn.'

'*What?*'

'You thought I had flu. Everyone did. Even me to begin with.' Lisa swallowed. 'I lost the baby before I even knew I was going to have one. That's a laugh, isn't it?'

'Oh, Lisa.'

Kit took her hand and held it. Lisa gave her a faint, tired smile.

'Well, Nikolai was away and when he came back he was furious. He said I wasn't being sensible. We had a terrible row.'

'And that was what was wrong at Coral Cove?' said Kit, enlightened.

Lisa nodded bleakly. 'For months it didn't seem as if we could stop arguing. We'd keep starting out to discuss it sensibly. And then one of us would fly off the handle and it would all start again. He said—he said I ought to give up my job. When I said no, he said I didn't deserve a child. That I wasn't maternal enough. I said— oh, I said a lot of nasty things. In the end we even stopped sleeping together.'

She drew a shaky sigh. Kit was silent, horrified at the turmoil she had not even guessed at.

'Coral Cove was supposed to be the chance to sort ourselves out. But Nikolai spent as little time with me as possible.'

'But—just before I left—you seemed so happy. I thought you were reconciled.'

'Sex,' said Lisa harshly. 'The great illusion.'

Kit flinched.

Lisa did not notice. 'Then it was back to square one as soon as we disagreed about something.'

'Me,' said Kit almost inaudibly.

Lisa shrugged. 'Whatever. He walked out, you know. Left me there.'

Kit was appalled. 'Did he know you were going to have a baby?'

Lisa shook her head. 'I didn't know myself then.'

'And now that he does?'

Lisa looked away.

'He does know, doesn't he?' Kit's voice rose. 'Lisa, you have told him?'

'I don't know how to get hold of him,' Lisa said defensively. 'He's up country somewhere. One of his beastly expeditions.'

Kit bit her lip. 'So what are you going to do?'

'Stay here with you?' Lisa looked up pleadingly. 'You'll help me through this, won't you, Kit? I mean, you're the maternal one...'

Kit was astonished. 'Am I?'

'Of course,' said Lisa as if it was common knowledge. Her hand twitched in Kit's. 'Help me,' she said in a low voice. 'I'm so *scared*, Kit.'

And Kit put her arms round her and said, 'I'll help you.'

It was a promise.

*　　*　　*

In the end it was quite easy. Kit supposed it always was if you knew the right people. Of course, until Philip she never had known the right people.

She did not know which hotel he was staying at in London. But she had a fair idea of how to contact his office, after her skirmish with his address book. Fernando, seeing a chance of redeeming himself in his chief's eyes, could not have been more helpful. He also told her that Philip was already on a plane.

So he had not even stayed in London for the three nights that were theoretically left to them! Kit tried not to let that hurt. She wanted a means of contacting her brother-in-law, after all.

Philip's assistant provided that with astonishing rapidity. The address was already in his database.

And, sure enough, that evening Nikolai was on the telephone.

It took him three days to get back. But he was on the telephone every chance he had, from scrubby hotels and ferry stations and airports. By the time he walked in, unshaven and dangerous, it felt as if he had been imminent forever.

Lisa went into his arms like a homing pigeon.

'My darling, my darling,' said Nikolai.

And said nothing else for some considerable time.

Kit fled.

It was not just a question of leaving them alone. The look on Nikolai's face had shaken her. She could not imagine Philip would ever look at her like that. Not that Philip would ever appear anyway with three days' growth of beard. Or lose control like that, she thought sadly.

Eventually Lisa emerged from her dreamy fog.

'How clever of you to find him,' she said, not letting go of Nikolai's hand. 'How did you do it?'

Kit muttered. But between them they dragged it out of her.

'Philip Hardesty?' said Nikolai incredulously. 'You had *Philip Hardesty's* office in New York jumping through hoops just to get hold of me?'

'Well, Lisa needed you.'

He exchanged looks with Lisa. 'That's not the point,' he said at last drily.

Kit was puzzled. 'So?'

'It sounds as if Philip Hardesty told his people that you were special,' explained Lisa kindly.

'Oh.' Kit flushed. 'Not that special,' she said painfully.

More of that wordless communication between husband and wife.

Then Lisa said airily, 'One of those. I see. A no-commitment kind of guy.'

'No.' Kit was surprised at how indignant she felt on Philip's behalf. 'No, he's committed all right. For life. To duty. To his job. He doesn't think he can ask any woman to share it.'

Nikolai said quietly, 'And what do you think?'

Kit's expression answered for her.

Nikolai looked at Lisa again. He said, 'I think you've got to do something about this, Kit.'

The night was loud with jungle noises. Kit heard them with her heart in her mouth. Pelanang did not have Coral Cove's civilised attitude to the taming of the tropics. This was ninety per cent humidity, with mosquitoes the size of toy helicopters and an airstrip hacked out from tree cover that threatened to block out the stars.

Kit would have been afraid if she hadn't been even more afraid of what Philip was going to say when he came back from his foray into the guerrillas' camp and found her. For Nikolai, getting her ticketed, immunised and visa-ed, had provided her with everything except what she was going to say to Philip.

So Kit stayed at Pelanang and tried out various gambits while she waited in the rough settlement.

'Give me a chance?' Too pathetic.

'Marry me?' Too ambitious.

'Love me?' Downright hopeless.

Now it was night. She was too hot to sleep in her corrugated-iron hut and too lonely to bear her own thoughts. So she had walked up the river a little way, keeping her flashlight carefully focused and sticking to the path, in her high-sided boots.

She knew what to do now. She had learned enough jungle lore not to be a danger to herself or anyone else. She had even become quite a pet of the tired administrators running the communications centre. She was pleased with herself for learning the skills and with them for respecting her. But she was still so *lonely*.

There was only one person who would ever stop her being lonely, thought Kit. And she had not the slightest idea what to say to him.

There was the sound of boots on the mud path. She flinched. Her instinct was to dive into the bushes and wait until this intruder had gone. But she knew that would be foolhardy. Jungle plants could give you a nasty rash, if not worse, and there were poisonous creatures everywhere. So she stood her ground and turned the flashlight on the newcomer.

And...

And...

Philip said, 'There's no need to blind me.'

It was him. It was *him*. So tall, so composed, so elegant—

Kit looked closer. Not so elegant. He had three days' growth of beard on that immaculate jaw. And not so composed either. Not from the rate at which his chest was rising and falling.

He stopped dead, a little distance from her on the path, and said, 'Thank God you're safe, Kit. I've been every kind of a fool. If you'd been hurt—'

'Why should I be hurt?' said Kit, bewildered.

His laugh broke. 'Spiders. Snakes. Goddamn man-eating orchids. Hell, how should I know? All I could think of was you here in the middle of the jungle and me not with you. Don't ever do that to me again, Kit. Please.'

The flashlight fell in her hands. 'I don't understand.'

He came up to her then. 'No. I know. I'm doing this all wrong. Kit, I know I didn't ask you when I should have done. But marry me.' He sounded frantic.

Kit stared and stared. Was this cool, controlled Philip Hardesty who weighed every word and always said the right thing, turning up unheralded, on a spontaneous impulse, and blurting out a proposal of *marriage*?

She said hopefully, 'You don't mean that.'

He groaned. 'Yes, I do. Deep down, I've meant it since the moment I met you. Though it's taken me too long to realise it. Don't you remember I told you I'd poison any member of my family who tried to marry you?'

'That was a joke.'

'Jokes are a way of telling the truth.'

Kit began to tremble.

He took her hands, flashlight and all. 'Have you ever felt about anyone the way you feel about me?

She cried out. 'That's not fair.'

'I've never been fair to you. Doesn't that tell you something? I'm always fair. I'm fair to tyrants and murderers. Just—not you.' He touched her cheek fleetingly, as if he was afraid she would push him away. 'You're the other half of myself. And I treated you like dirt.' He sounded furious with himself.

Kit said gently, 'No, you didn't. You could see that I'm not up to your standards, that's all.'

'Don't you dare say that.'

'But it's true.' She was distracted by his nearness, by her unpreparedness, by her *need*. She babbled, 'I'm not properly educated. I have weird hang-ups. I don't know my ancestors. And I could never keep a tiara on.'

He held her away from him and stared into her face. In the flashlight her expression was naked.

He said incredulously, 'You really believe that nonsense.'

Kit's eyes fell.

'Oh, those eyelashes,' he said on a shaken breath.

She looked up. 'What?'

Philip pulled himself together. 'Your education is purpose-built. By you. Nothing wrong with it. I didn't notice any hang-ups.' His eyes glinted wickedly. 'Ancestors I can live without. You'll learn to balance a tiara. Anything else?'

Kit said uncertainly, 'You're laughing at me.'

'At you? God forbid.'

And suddenly he was so serious that she flinched.

'At Ashbarrow—when we were together—I felt complete,' he said. He did not sound as if he was finding it easy. Philip Hardesty, fluent diplomat, was groping for words. 'You showed me things—things about my own home, places I knew—that I'd never seen before. You made me laugh. And you made me burn. And you made me want to be different.'

Kit was silenced. She felt humbled.

Philip said in a low voice, 'And I do want to be different, Kit. You were right. I was afraid love would weaken me. I don't want to be like that any more.'

She did not know what to say. She moved close to him, feeling his dear, familiar body under her hands, and knew that he was hers and she was his. But she still did not know what to say.

He said painfully, 'Your godmother said something to me, you know. She said, "She always wanted to heal things, my Kit."'

Kit's eyes were pricking with tears. 'R-really?'

He bent his head until his brow rested on her hair.

His voice was a thread. 'Heal *me*, Kit.'

The jungle rattled and hissed and sweated all about them. All she could hear was his pulse and hers, their ragged breathing, and their unspoken desire.

She found she knew what to say after all. 'Do you love me?'

He raised his head and looked deep into her eyes. 'I love you,' he said.

'Then I will marry you.'

'Oh, Kit,' he said, dragging her against him so hard that her ribs felt as if they would crack. 'Sweet, sensible, wonderful Kit. Who would believe I could get this lucky?'

But she was not listening. She was pulling his head down for her kiss—and to tell him what he had not asked.

'I love you, Philip. I may get worried about you when you're away. But I won't let it get me down.' It was a fierce whisper. 'And I'll wear that damned tiara if it kills me.'

He laughed aloud. Then kissed her until her head swam. And then, raising his head, announced to the jungle night, 'We can handle it together.'

EPILOGUE

It was another of those impromptu Press conferences.

The journalists were pleased. The photographs of the guerrillas who had just rejoined the peace talks looked suitably villainous. The pile of surrendered weapons was impressive. And the chief negotiator was being unusually co-operative for once.

'And you will continue to run the negotiations, Sir Philip?' asked one of the trusted agency correspondents, encouraged by this exceptional good humour. 'There were rumours about your health.'

'No, I shall stick with it to the end,' Philip said cheerfully. 'It's true I had an eye problem.' He smiled at someone in the crowd. 'It seems to have cleared up over the last few days.'

'Do you ever regret doing the job you do?' asked the local stringer. With all these hot-shot international correspondents around, the only chance he had of filing a story was to go for the human-interest angle. 'It must be a lonely life.'

At the edge of the hot little room Captain Soames and Texas Joe winked at each other. And Philip Hardesty broke into a full-scale grin.

'Not in the immediate future,' he said. 'I stopped off in Coral Cove again.' It had been an easy decision. Hardly any decision at all. There would be family and friends to tell, and the party of the century to hold in the future. Now they just needed to be together. 'Only this time I got married.'

He held out his hand. Kit went to him. He put his arm round her and kissed her, unashamed, in front of all those cameras.

'Gentlemen,' he said proudly, 'my wife.'

MILLS & BOON® PUBLISH EIGHT LARGE PRINT TITLES A MONTH. THESE ARE THE EIGHT TITLES FOR JUNE 2002

A SECRET VENGEANCE
Miranda Lee

THE ITALIAN'S BRIDE
Diana Hamilton

D'ALESSANDRO'S CHILD
Catherine Spencer

DESERT AFFAIR
Kate Walker

THE ENGAGEMENT EFFECT
Neels & Fielding

THE ENGLISHMAN'S BRIDE
Sophie Weston

THE BRIDEGROOM'S VOW
Rebecca Winters

THE WEDDING DARE
Barbara Hannay

MILLS & BOON®

Makes any time special™

MILLS & BOON® PUBLISH EIGHT LARGE PRINT TITLES A MONTH. THESE ARE THE EIGHT TITLES FOR JULY 2002

THE SECRET LOVE-CHILD
Miranda Lee

AN ARABIAN MARRIAGE
Lynne Graham

THE SPANIARD'S SEDUCTION
Anne Mather

THE GREEK TYCOON'S BRIDE
Helen Brooks

THE BOSS'S DAUGHTER
Leigh Michaels

THE BABY QUESTION
Caroline Anderson

HIS SECRETARY'S SECRET
Barbara McMahon

A SPANISH HONEYMOON
Anne Weale

MILLS & BOON®